THE MAULER

THE RAVAGER WAR PREQUEL

C.A. GLEASON

Cover art by Darko Tomic

ISBN: 9798355857196

PART 1

Planet Tuhrelevim

CHAPTER 1

The vociferous whir of the gyrating blades whined, a reliable platform for Staff Sergeant Ryan's thoughts. With earplugs in, he barely deciphered it anymore.

The choppy resounding rotor of the Adelpa HJC was almost soothing in its familiarity, a rare loud noise that nearly disappeared from his hearing while he was forced to focus on everything else.

"What if we fail, sir?" Sergeant Burbano asked.

Captain Swain sighed. "*We* fail, *they* send probes."

"Yes, sir." Burbano said as he leaned over to Tower, "But if they send probes, we'll never know."

Sergeant Tower scoffed. "Optimist. And don't say the F-word."

Burbano squinted. "I didn't."

"Failure."

Ryan was on the other side of Tower. "Good thing the F-word isn't an option for Iron Sights Squad."

"Got that right," Tower agreed.

Private Slater put a hand to the side of her mouth. "Fuckin' A right!"

Tower's helmeted head twisted above his LBV (load bearing vest). "Save that motivation for when our boots are on the ground, Private."

Slater pushed a strand of hair into a helmet that looked too big for her. "Yes, Sergeant."

"I was just messing with everybody," Burbano said. "Failure can go fuck itself. Got my weapon. Got my clips. I'm good to go. *We're* good to go."

"Did you say clips?" Tower asked. "You meant magazines,

right?"

"Clip sounds cooler."

"Maybe but it's wrong. You sound like a civilian."

"Whatever. What's the name of this planet again?"

"You're on a roll. Really? It's Tuhrelevim."

"Tuh—*say again*?"

"*Tuh-rel-eh-vim*. Tuhrelevim."

"Yeah, like that's going to stick. They couldn't pick something that wasn't dumb? Or that can be pronounced."

"Too easy if you can read."

"*Tuh*-irrelevant is more like it."

Ryan had to laugh and it caught on. Except for Private Moss, who remained stoic, and used to be a staff sergeant.

Moss held a sniper rifle and was a shadow having applied camouflage paint to her face and hands. She disappeared among her fellow soldiers every time she blinked. Seemed the sniper was anxious to get boots on the ground too.

Ryan had to force himself to ignore how pretty Moss was. Her short, dark hair drew attention to her sharp features even more.

The pilot's voice squelched over the radios on their shoulders. *"None of you want to see what's beneath us. They are wicked looking. Yikes."*

Ryan looked up at Tower. "Yikes?"

Tower leaned over. "I think yikes is bad."

"Why does that make me want to see them even more?" Specialist Newlin said.

"You're our medic," Private First Class Page said. "Shouldn't you be the sanest of us? Concentrate."

"Thanks, Private," Newlin said.

"You're welcome, Specialist," Page said.

"Chief," Ryan called out to the pilot. "How close were they when we—"

Chief Warrant Officer McGary replied, *"Too close."*

Seemed they'd made the transformation from jet to helicopter, requiring landing—for inexperienced pilots, Ryan had heard—just in time.

Some pilots could transform an A-brid from jet mode to helicopter mode from high elevation according to a few drunks at the bar on base.

The wheels could be extended if a hover skiff or some other vehicle was attached underneath the fuselage, but for their first potential combat mission on the planet, it was Adelpa HJC—a.k.a A-brid—only.

Ryan remembered having the feeling they were being watched while guarding the brief perimeter they'd established during the switch. Apparently, the A-brid had taken off just in time to avoid the wildlife.

And soon after, while airborne, they'd wisely shut the door and kept it closed. Too much of a chance for something unknown to get in.

If anything does get through the door, it's going to have to go through all of us, Ryan thought.

"Are they predators or prey?" Burbano asked.

"Do you think I'd be paranoid about herds of herbivores?" McGary said. *"Speaking of, they're ravaging one of them right now. Yep, just tore it to pieces."*

"Great," Ryan said.

"I swear the one with the bloodiest mouth is staring at me," McGary said. *"Either it hates me or my bird."*

"Don't you mean brid?" Ryan said. "Adelpa HJCs are called A-brids for short after all."

"Thank you, Sergeant Ryan. My brid. I like that better and I'm stealing it."

"You're welcome."

"It hates my face or my brid. Anyhow, we're being hunted."

"Thanks for that, Chief," Burbano said. "You're scaring me."

"*Us*," Tower said.

"Chief," Swain said. "Will you report that to higher please?"

"Wilco."

"Seems pretty obvious what happened to the explorers," Newlin said. "We can head home now, sir?"

"Very funny, Specialist," Swain said.

"Explorers," Tower said. "Is that what we're calling colonists these days?"

"What they're called is irrelevant, Sergeant," Lieutenant Bates said.

Tower kept his mouth shut, but Ryan suspected it was difficult for him. Rank alone didn't automatically command respect, the man or woman wearing it did, and Sergeant Tower and Lieutenant Bates already didn't like each other.

Probably because they were similar in a way. One of Tower's many strengths was strength, and according to Bates's file, his strength was smarts. Sometimes strengths collided.

There were a few tense moments as the aircraft continued to control the airspace, piloted by McGary, but the two men relaxed, allowing the rest of the squad to do the same.

Even with all of the forests and mountains on the alien planet, the A-brid was like a giant insect that could land anywhere it wanted, and rumbled with confidence. Who knew how far the sound of it resounded.

The A-brid hadn't been on very many flights yet, and neither had humans been on the planet long.

Until humans dominated the planet—that was the plan—they would be considered the aliens. That had been in the briefing. Everyone on board, back at base, and those in transit, understood that.

And they'd also been made to understand it in writing.

CHAPTER 2

Captain Swain had ordered that there be no consumption of alcohol the day before the mission. Everyone needed to be tip-top.

Ryan could have used a few drinks to take the edge off. Families would begin arriving from those large Adelpa 4 transport ships soon.

Ryan was single. His previous relationship ended when his girlfriend decided not to marry him right before deploying to an uncharted planet.

Maybe she was the smart one.

He didn't have to look after anyone but himself and his squad, but there was still concern on his part of course. No one talked about it but accidents happened.

Fortunately, there were no transportation accidents so far, just people on the planet going missing.

Death or going missing was possible because it had happened already, but it was still a thrill to be first. The first round in the chamber as Ryan and his fellow soldiers liked to say.

Being the first round in the chamber was risky, and it would be a lonely deployment for Ryan, unless he met someone.

And how often does it take only one bullet to accomplish a mission?

But the future was uncertain, he must remember.

Figuratively, Ryan was keeping his head down, focused on the mission, and did his best to ignore how much money he was making since it would be useless to him if he didn't live to spend it.

There were other single soldiers—like Moss, as far as he knew. He would think about dating when he returned to base.

No alcohol but they were allowed coffee. Not since liftoff, of course.

Shortly after the briefing, Colonel Horne had told Ryan he should quit drinking alcohol because it dulled the senses, and that he should switch to coffee. Ryan told the colonel he drank coffee already. Horne found that amusing.

Ryan nearly mentioned that getting senses dulled was kind of the point of drinking alcohol, but he didn't want to antagonize the senior officer if he could help it, so he just thanked him for the advice.

There had been constant small talk between the soldiers and also laughter, and Swain whispered something to Bates.

"Stifle it," Bates said.

After giving the quiet command to Bates, one Ryan recognized without hearing—to keep the soldiers focused—the squad on board had done enough joking according to Captain Swain.

To Ryan's annoyance.

Officers rarely understood the grunts. Allowing them to joke around ensured they'd be mission ready when the mission really started. It didn't really matter how they were during the flight.

An officer who was a rare exception, who understood grunts well, was Captain Nev, and that was why, given the choice, Ryan would have preferred Captain Nev to be leading the mission over Captain Swain.

Ryan didn't have anything against Swain personally, but Swain was one of those officers who tended to stay on board instead of putting his boots on the ground first. The squad knew it too. They'd gossiped about it and Ryan had ordered them to stop.

A man like Captain Nev never hesitated to be the first round in the chamber and lead the way, just like everyone on board who wasn't to be saluted. Ryan wished Nev was stationed there already.

One of the soldiers who Ryan was glad to have on mission and aboard was Sergeant Tower. Tower exemplified everything the military wanted in a soldier; focus, obedience, reliability, and dependability.

And also, natural improvisational skills between an order given and mission accomplished. Ryan had even joked to him that he should be cloned.

Tower resisted promotion because he'd rather remain in the thick of missions—or a firefight—than be a leader. The irony was how everyone wanted to follow him anyway. He was a natural leader.

Except the officers on board are oblivious to that fact.

Perhaps in time, Tower would change his mind about promotion. A soldier like him was good for morale and for the military. In Ryan's opinion, he'd make Sergeant Major one day whether he wanted to or not.

Tower was experienced but still young, in his mid-twenties. Not an old man like Ryan, who was in his late-twenties.

"Tower," Ryan said, "how much coffee do you have on you?"

"The add it to boiled water that's perfect for training or a mission. That kind? None of your business."

"I saw you pack your ruck."

"Then why ask? Get your own."

"I have my own."

"Well, you're not getting any of mine so be disciplined about yours."

The lieutenant frowned, giving Ryan the look now. Ryan knew how much to joke around himself before he'd be told to stifle it. He'd been a private before, and he'd be told the same way Bates spoke to the others of low rank. If Ryan kept it up.

But everyone was up in their heads. The flight was taking longer than expected. Alien planet, what were they really doing there, people missing or dead and no one knew the details and all that.

Ryan still joked around when he was nervous, even though he'd been enlisted for years and hadn't been a private for a long time.

No matter how many missions he went on, he still felt that cocktail of excitement and nervousness at the same time. It still spilled out his mouth sometimes, regardless of his rank, even as a staff sergeant.

Ryan was lucky Tower was part of the squad, that he was willing to take the same risk they all were by going, being stationed on the planet at all. Tower had taken some convincing by Ryan himself, and quite a few drinks.

With Tower on the mission, not only did they have a soldier along who was one of the best at soldiering, but his presence kept the others in line, including Ryan.

Tower's rank was one lower than Ryan's, but Tower achieved the standard and essentially kept the bar out of reach. The rest of them could only reach for it or exhaust themselves jumping for it.

Tower kept them better than they actually were.

CHAPTER 3

PFC Moss insisted on going along for the mission because she'd insisted, they'd need her. Ryan had agreed to make room for the former staff sergeant and that sniper rifle of hers.

Moss got annoyed if there was a better path to mission success that was suggested but it was ignored.

She'd been busted down to private for suggesting an alternate path to accomplish a certain mission, and then went outside the wire against orders to make it happen.

If Moss regretted her decision, she didn't show it, and was slowly working her way back up in rank again.

After losing her rank, Moss had been assigned to Iron Sights Squad, but because she was only a private—PFC now—the sniper had been teased that she wasn't truly a member of the squad because her weapon was often equipped with a scope.

Until she bested those who talked shit to her while on the firing range, shooting their weapons better than they did, using only iron sights and at battle sight zero. There was no more teasing after that.

Moss studied each member of the squad like a predator hunting prey. Ryan thought Moss's face even resembled a bird of prey with her pointy nose and chin. She rarely spoke now unless spoken to. She'd probably get chattier as she ascended in rank.

Tower smirked. "You need a hug or something?"

Ryan pretended like he hadn't been lost in thought. "Just admiring you is all."

"I'm flattered."

"You should be."

Ryan ignored the look he was getting from Bates and also Swain.

Ignored what either of them might say next; "stifle it," or "let's stay on mission."

Ryan had been testing Bates. He wanted to know his irritation threshold, something that could be very telling under pressure, and also useful. And Ryan had assessed Bates's sense of humor; he didn't have one.

"Hey, Sergeant," Newlin said. "You can have some of my coffee if you want. If you run out."

"Thanks, Specialist," Ryan said. "I would have taken it from you anyway but at least you offered."

Newlin chuckled, popped a gum bubble, and continued staring across from him. At Page.

"Quit staring," Page said.

"You wish," Newlin said, flipping him off.

"No man, you wish."

"That's enough," Bates said.

Ryan smirked. At least it wasn't the captain. The second in command glared at Newlin, then Page, and then even Sergeant Burbano for some reason.

Burbano mirrored his glare. "Help you with something, sir?"

Bates reacted as if Burbano had told him to jump ship. The lieutenant made everyone nervous, even more than Swain did. He'd only been a member of the squad since arriving on the planet, a short period of time.

He was a member of the squad, but not considered one of them by any of them. Not even among the few squad members who didn't go on the mission, who were in the rear with the gear. In fact, Bates looked nervous to be in his own skin.

"Are you disrespecting me, Sergeant?"

"Negative, sir," Burbano said. "I simply asked if I could help you with something."

"When I need anything from you or your fellow soldiers, I'll inform you. Just focus on the mission."

"Yes, sir."

Burbano definitely wanted to tell Bates where to go.

But instead of saying anything, Tower spoke up for him. "We're on the same side, sir."

"Tell me something I don't know, Sergeant Tower."

"You're not acting like it, sir."

The captain's brow furrowed. "Sergeant Tower . . . Chief McGary, how far away are we from Fort Beckett?"

McGary said, *"About a thousand klicks."*

"That's how many pushups you all owe Lieutenant Bates for a disrespectful tone. Unless you'd like to do them all yourself, Tower."

"I would, sir."

"No time like the present."

"I agree, sir."

Tower unbuckled his safety harness, laid his weapon on his seat, dropped, and started doing pushups.

The captain is an idiot, too, Ryan thought. *Is he trying to splinter the squad?*

"What are you all waiting for?" Ryan said.

He dropped down next to Tower, the rest did too, and they started knocking out 1000 pushups, one at a time, together.

"Just like basic training," Slater said.

"Gotta love group punishment," Page said.

"Anything else makes us soft," Newlin said.

"One thousand each or combined?" Burbano asked.

"You're hilarious," Ryan said.

"Care to join us, sir?" Tower asked as he pushed up and down like a machine.

Bates glared down at him.

CHAPTER 4

Burbano grinned at the door, where they'd be stepping out once it was unlocked and slid open after landing. "What's our ETA, sir?"

Bates opened his mouth to answer, but Swain talked over him. "Chief?"

Bates was not amused, but Burbano was.

McGary adjusted the mic attached to his helmet. *"Thirty mics."*

"Hear that, Sergeant?" Swain asked.

"Got it, sir," Burbano said.

Bates seemed intent on having a staring contest against Burbano, but Burbano looked away first, shaking his head.

Bates seemed stuck on figuring out a way to antagonize Burbano, to get back at him, often an abuse of power young officers liked to take advantage of. Ryan had seen it a thousand times.

Swain cut short anything he was about to spout with a curt, "Lieutenant."

Bates relaxed and sat back. All they wanted to do was get there, Ryan knew. Get to it, get it on if necessary. Even Bates.

Sometimes soldiers were so ready for a mission that they'd turn on their own. Most of the time it was just arguing.

They were a long way from base. They were on an alien planet but it might as well have been an alien planet's moon.

All of it was practically unknown, no matter how familiar the terrain looked in comparison to Earth, and where humans originated.

In less than thirty minutes—most likely—they'd touch down for the first of multiple searches, until the explorers were located, or their fate was discovered.

It was up to Swain to decide how many times they would touch down before flying back to base, but there was only so much fuel.

"Chief," Burbano said. "Are those predators still down there?"

McGary leaned in the cockpit, looking out the window on his left. *"Negative. We cleared them. They must have lost interest in us."*

Burbano tilted his head and cracked his neck. "Good."

Ryan squeezed the handle of the Rovla assault rifle through his tactical gloves, as soothing and as comfortable as laying his head on a clean pillow to catch some z's.

He used to prefer holding a weapon bare handed but everyone else wore gloves, and even though he didn't have to, he wanted to blend in with the rest, and now he was used to it.

Being a team player was out of habit. Standing out in the military could be a one-way ticket to an eventual discharge, and taking steps not to get discharged was also out of habit. The best way to do that was to seek uniformity.

Once Ryan was promoted, rank by rank, he'd start doing what he wanted to do more and more, as he'd noticed men like Colonel Horne do, and think for himself.

Wearing tactical gloves was one of the few comforts afforded collectively. He preferred wearing them now, but even if he didn't want to, he would have. Aside from Bates, they felt like a real team.

Burbano retied his right boot out of boredom. "Why is it that explorers are always going off and getting themselves lost."

"It's in their nature," Tower said. "They're like children without parents."

"So, savage little monsters?"

"Everyone gets lost eventually," Bates said.

There was snickering. Bates must have noticed the reaction.

"As I'm relatively new to the squad, its nickname . . ." Bates eyed the soldiers of lower rank; Page, Newlin, and Slater. "Is it as transparent as it seems?"

"It is," Tower answered for them.

And it was. A soldier in Iron Sights Squad was basic on requirements. Hardly any extra anything. No scope unless it was a sniper rifle. Rails were often bare. Just a weapon, ammo for that weapon, and essential supplies.

And with that, a perfect mission success rate.

Newlin smiled. “No attachments whatsoever, sir.”

“Give over your coffee then. All of you seemed to be obsessed with it. A weakness in my opinion.”

Don’t fall for the dig. Bates just wants to blow more smoke. 1000 pushups were enough for this mission.

“No soldier is perfect, sir,” Newlin said. “Coffee is mission fuel.”

“And you’re the medic.” Bates *tsked*. “That’s why Colonel Horne sent all of you?”

“Sent us, sir,” Tower said.

“You seem proud of needing so little. Perhaps you shouldn’t be. Perhaps you’re disillusioned. I myself need only calories, water, a weapon—”

“Lieutenant,” Swain said.

Bates smirked. “Understood, sir.”

“Fly overs,” Burbano complained. “Infinite fly overs.”

Tower egged him on. “Don’t forget circles. We’re not heading as the crow flies.”

“There’s nobody out here.” Burbano shook his head. “Nobody down there. Not anymore. We can all tell that, right?”

Ryan wasn’t the only one who wanted to reach their destination. The problem was they’d already reached it, except the destination wasn’t exactly known, only the area. Captain Swain seemed to be confused by the local terrain notifications.

The explorers disappeared around there somewhere.

Or maybe they didn’t.

Explorers tended to wander and take unnecessary chances. They were supposed to set marker flags but McGary hadn’t detected any. If they’d done it, then they hadn’t been placed where they were supposed to be.

Everything pointed to the explorers not being found, and Swain was not only reluctant to admit that, but also to command

McGary to land.

Except it was known that some of the explorers were ex-military and carried the same Rovla rifles the squad did. They had as good of a chance at survival as any soldier stationed there being armed, and hopefully some of them had.

Ryan knew something else, and what the rest of the squad didn't; there'd been artillery strikes already, but where they'd impacted, he didn't know.

When he'd started asking questions, Ryan quickly realized he'd overheard something he wasn't supposed to, based on the reaction. Colonel Horne had patiently told him it was classified.

All Ryan knew was that there was a lot more going on there than he cared to think about. And there was a lot more planned after they returned to base.

There were structures being built and some were already finished. He didn't know their purposes because he wasn't mission essential.

There were even rumors of aircraft crashes, military aircraft—before members of the squad had arrived—deemed classified too.

Maybe Ryan would do a little digging upon returning to base.

Currently, it was best for him to focus on the current mission.

"We're going to run out of fuel," Burbano said. "We should head back soon. What do you guys think?"

Tower laughed. "You think this is a democracy?"

"Stifle that, Sergeant Burbano," Swain said.

Burbano exhaled. "Yes, sir. It's just that we should have found at least traces of who's gone missing but there's nothing. Not even the marker flags they were supposed to set."

"That's true," Ryan said. "It is strange."

"The markers should be around here but they're not. Could the weather have knocked them down? I mean all of them?"

"And then destroyed them?" Ryan shook his head. "No way."

"Then what? Something took them?"

The rotor above *zipped* abnormally, before sounding normal again.

Tower's normally confident expression wavered. "What was

that? Chief?"

"Wait one."

"Something bounced off the blades," Page said. "That's what it felt like."

"Relax, Page," Ryan said.

"Yes, Sergeant. But what was it?"

"Nothing that can bring us down." Ryan had no idea if that were true but keeping his soldiers calm was his priority. "Probably one of those birds."

"Those aren't birds," Burbano said. "They don't fly like any birds I've ever seen."

"You've never seen birds," Tower said.

"Sure, I have."

"In pictures," Ryan said. "They fly. That's bird enough for me. I only get concerned when McGary does. Does he look concerned to you?"

Burbano twisted his head. "No, Sergeant."

Ryan nodded. "Thus, relax, Sergeant."

Burbano grinned. "Yes, Staff Sergeant."

CHAPTER 5

"I heard a few rumors." Slater waited.

Things were going wrong in a hurry. Swain still hadn't commanded a landing. They might not land at all, Ryan thought. And since the real mission had yet to begin, the soldiers were getting chatty again.

Neither officer seemed to care about that now. Swain was busily deciding if or where to touch down, obvious by the concerned look on his face, and Bates was looking to him to enforce any commands.

"I guess nobody cares, Private," Newlin said.

"Oh, OK, *Specialist*," Slater said. "I wasn't talking to you anyway."

"Liar."

"I want to know," Burbano said. "I'm curious."

"No, you don't, Sergeant," Newlin said. "Trust me."

"I trust myself, Specialist."

"Yeah, I do too," Page said.

Ryan glanced in the direction of the cockpit. The lieutenant looked like he had indigestion, and the captain looked just as annoyed. Ryan made eye contact with both of the officers and smirked.

Just let them talk. We've been in the air forever.

"Go ahead, Slater," Burbano said. "Once we hit the rank of Staff Sergeant, like Staff Sergeant Ryan and above, we can no longer gossip."

Ryan responded, "*Pfft*."

"OK," Slater said, "so, one day, anyone, and I mean *anyone*, will be able to fly one of these."

Burbano grimaced. "A-brids?"

"That's right, Sergeant."

"What are you talking about."

Slater nodded with a purpose. "Seriously."

"One of *these*."

"Yeah."

"This model."

"Well, no. But the next version. *A* next version, in the future. For civilians."

"For real?"

"True."

"No way," Page said.

Slater faced him. "Seriously."

"You're trying to tell us that civilians are going to pilot military aircraft?" Burbano asked.

"No," Slater said, "it would be like a dumbed down version."

"I don't believe it."

"What I'm getting at is there would hardly be any training necessary. Just jump in and fly."

Burbano shook his head. "That's impossible."

"I'm telling you they're working on some crazy stuff right now."

"Who's *they*?"

"You know, all those rich people with commas and zeroes in their bank accounts."

"Which rich people?"

"The ones footing the bill for our boots on the ground."

"Since when are privates privy to top secret? How do you know?"

"I heard it from somebody who heard it from somebody."

"But how do you know it's true?"

"I don't. It's just what I heard."

"She heard it because she's female," Page said. "And somebody had too many drinks at the bar."

"Whatever." Slater sighed. "Well, maybe, but I guess somebody's mad at the main guy who foots the bill, most of the bill, and talked. Told somebody who told somebody who told somebody who told me."

"That's a lot of somebodies," Tower said.

"Classified info spilled I guess," Slater said.

"Who told you?" Page asked.

Slater grinned. "That's classified."

"Fine. Who's the main guy?"

"I'll give you a hint. His name is on this aircraft."

"Hmm. What a riddle."

"Don't strain your brain."

"Seriously, who'd you hear it from?"

"You don't believe me?"

"If it came from a reliable source, I'll feel more comfortable passing it on."

"Someone around base."

"Well, no kidding. What was his rank?"

"Honestly, I don't remember."

"Yeah, sure."

"Seriously. You know how you hear stuff but can't remember where?"

"Yeah."

"It's like that."

"You sure you're OK?"

"A lot of soldiers buy me a lot of drinks when we're off duty. Leave me alone."

"See that's your mistake, Slater," Newlin said. "You can't be left alone to drink yourself stupid until you've attained the rank of Specialist or above."

Slater had a smile like she had as many commas and zeroes in her bank account as could be imagined. "Who said I drank myself stupid?"

"Cunning, Private. Cunning," Newlin said. "What are you going to do with all of those top secrets?"

"Sell them to the highest bidder." Slater reacted to Swain and Bates looking in her direction. "Only kidding, Gentlemen!" When they looked away from her, she mouthed, "I'm not kidding."

"You'd better be," Ryan said.

Slater's smile straightened. "Yes, Sergeant. I am."

CHAPTER 6

"First rounds in the chamber," Newlin said. "Figures. Why us?"

"Round in the chamber," Tower corrected.

"Say again, Sergeant?"

"Only one round in the chamber at a time, Specialist."

Ryan smiled at that.

"Whatever, Sergeant," Newlin said. "I mean . . . we can't all be one round, we're different soldiers. Thus rounds. I was being inclusive."

"How thoughtful of you." Tower smirked. "So, we're a bunch of individuals? I thought we were a squad."

"Fine, Sergeant. Round in the chamber. First round in the chamber. My point stands. Why us?"

"Actually," Ryan said, "it's because of Sergeant Tower."

"Me?"

"Yeah, you. Don't pretend like you don't enjoy going on missions."

"And you don't?"

"Not as much as you. Nobody does."

"Higher thinks so. Not my fault."

"Of course, it is," Burbano said. "And now that I think about it you do. You volunteer for everything."

"So?"

"So, you volunteer, you volunteer us, *hero*."

Ryan put a hand to the side of his mouth even though they were right next to each other. "Thanks a lot, Tower."

Tower elbowed him. "I set the standard. What else am I going to do."

"Ow," Ryan said. "You do like going on missions, though, right?"

"What do you think?" Tower put his Rovla in his left hand, barrel pointed at the floor, and flexed a bicep as large around as most of their waists. "Hey, Burbano, what else would you be doing?"

"Joking in the rear."

"You do enough of that. Your rank is too high now. Course correct or else."

"Not according to our trusty medic. According to him, you have to at least reach staff sergeant before you gotta stop acting like a knucklehead."

Something punched the side of the A-brid and their world tilted.

"That was an impact," Bates said. "Chief McGary, what is happening? I thought you said animals were no longer beneath us."

"The packs of them aren't. But I think a lone one jumped from a tree or something. It just hit the side. But there's no damage. None that I can tell. Everything remains functional."

"And you didn't think that information would benefit the rest of us on board?"

"It just happened. I don't answer to you, Bates!"

McGary's voice sounded from the speakers on their shoulders, but he'd sounded off loud enough to be heard without them.

The last thing they needed was an argument, and Ryan was skilled at defusing them early. "Are there any animals moving beneath us, Chief?"

"Chief," Swain said, leaning toward him, and pointing. "Is it wise to fly so close to those hills?"

"Let me do my job, Captain—oh shit!"

A shadow engulfed the A-brid.

Whatever it was, it passed in front of the sun, and the gyrating blades chopped it to pieces.

Right afterward, an alarm blared while indistinguishable voices shouted commands and everything leaned while falling.

CHAPTER 7

The world spun, even while Ryan got his bearings. Seconds felt like minutes, and getting himself together took concentration. He wondered if he'd hit his head, and was glad he'd been wearing a helmet.

He looked around. Of the survivors, they all still wore them.

The one thing he wished was still spinning were the rotor blades of the A-brid. But all of it was in pieces, obvious as the rest of the aircraft had cracked open to flood in the world.

Most of the aircraft was relatively intact after the crash. They had been flying at a low elevation and it had saved their lives. Except for the captain.

Ryan felt like he might be in pieces too, but it didn't feel like anything was broken. His arms and legs and neck throbbed.

Strained, maybe even sprained—both ankles were sore—but he wasn't injured too badly. He could still think straight.

Captain Swain was dead even though he'd been wearing a helmet too. What could be seen of his face was punctured with bits of metal. He was also bent at the waist in a way showing there were no signs of life.

He'd been closest to the cockpit and killed upon impact. That didn't prevent the medic, Newlin, from attempting to inspect Swain's injuries.

With a grimace, he finally accepted that the captain was deceased, so he searched for anyone else who might require medical attention.

Everyone else seems uninjured, even our medic.

Bates stared vacantly. Possibly a head injury. He'd removed his helmet after the crash. When Newlin tried to get a better look at a scalp wound—a mystery—Bates caught his hand and threw it away.

Bates glared down at Swain's corpse, no doubt understanding that he was now in command.

The sound of the planet was alive and enveloping, with bugs flitting about, but most of them unseen and buzzing.

Mountains surrounded them. Snow could be seen on the highest peaks.

Ryan hadn't noticed the mountains during the ride on the A-brid. It had been purposeful. He tried only to appreciate the beauty of terrain once they were returning from training, a mission, or while on base.

There was tall, green grass everywhere. Fields of it stretched as far as the eye could see, to the horizon, leading to endless hills. A valley led to tall, dark mountains.

Creepy.

Other than the wreckage, and the scorched and blackened ground in the vicinity of the crash due to burning, it looked like they'd crashed in paradise.

At least none of it was still on fire. Tower had sprayed down flames with the fire extinguisher he'd found.

"Who is hurt?" Ryan asked. "Who is injured?"

No one complained. Moss looked the same as she did while in flight and blended in with the background even more now, and somehow more than the others with her natural demeanor.

Newlin walked around in tight circles with a noticeable limp. It seemed he was trying to figure it out.

"Newlin?"

"Slight sprain, Sergeant. I think. But I'm good to go."

"Is it swollen?"

"Somewhat. But I can walk. And I'll keep my boot on."

"If anything changes, I want to know about it. Pay attention to the swelling next time you change your socks. Especially if you can't get your boot back on."

"Yes, Sergeant."

Tower set down the extinguisher. "I'm good to go."

Ryan inspected his battle buddies. There were lines of red on faces but nothing that looked too severe. They all looked well enough given what had happened. Based on the destruction of the crash, they were lucky to have survived.

"Everyone else, OK?" Ryan asked. "Or OK enough? Sir?"

Bates's glare lifted from Swain's corpse to Ryan. "I told you I was fine, Sergeant."

"Actually, you didn't say anything to me, sir."

"I'm fine, Sergeant."

Doesn't seem that way. "Good to know."

Ryan tried inspecting everyone more closely—soldiers tended to be too proud to complain about simple aches and pains—noticing everyone but Bates was looking to Ryan as if he were in charge.

But that was the way it typically went when missions went south. When the shit hit the fan, everyone tended to look to who was best for guidance, regardless of rank. Sometimes officers, but often not.

Ryan would allow himself to take command, even though any reports to higher would show the lieutenant as being in charge.

He eyed the pilot and gave him a questioning thumbs up. McGary gave him one in return.

CHAPTER 8

It was strange seeing so much of what was just airborne in pieces. Not the bulk of it, or they'd all be dead, but what had destructed seemed impossible because—other than Captain Swain—the rest of them had survived.

Parts of the A-brid that had come loose were flattened, torn, shredded, or burned. Some of it still smoked. There was no sign of the wings when in jet formation—before or after an A-brid transformed into a helicopter.

Plumes of smoke encompassed what could be seen of the mast, the part of the rotor that was the most intact.

The rotor blades had splintered, sending sharp pieces of metal everywhere, glinting in the sun in random places. Because of where the A-brid had cracked open, that was likely what had killed Swain.

The rest of us are lucky to be alive.

"Page," Ryan said, "comms status?"

"We knew it was a risk this far out. In a couple of months, established antennas will hopefully allow reliable communication intervals."

"Hopefully? That's optimistic," Burbano said. "Realistically, it'll take years."

"OK," Ryan said. "So, we can't depend on extended comms out here?"

"I don't think so," Page said. "Not for this mission, Sergeant. We can communicate through our shoulder radios but that's it. Sorry."

"Not your fault, Private."

It was like having no communications at all since they didn't plan on getting separated, and would only communicate through their shoulder radios if they had to.

So, what is the mission now?

They were nearly a thousand miles away from base. And with no direct communication with Fort Beckett.

Not until they were closer anyway. Ryan compartmentalized that part of the mission in his mind and stowed it temporarily.

Burbano applied a field dressing to his wrist and instantly it darkened. "Why is it that whenever missions go badly, they go in a big way."

Bates already wasn't doing his job according to his rank. That wasn't just Ryan's opinion, it was fact, because he was a statue.

Ryan would be better for command until Bates snapped out of it. Until the lieutenant stepped up, Ryan decided he would assume the role.

Commanders needed to give commands as much as soldiers needed missions. Page was the RTO (radio transmitter operator), and there were only basic communications. He must have felt useless. He needed a mission.

"Page, strip the captain of all necessary gear," Ryan ordered.

"That's OK, Sergeant," Slater said. "I'm closer to him. Shall I go ahead?"

Ryan was surprised. "Affirmative."

Slater went about the difficult task of removing Swain's weapons, ammo, and canteens.

Ryan imagined it wasn't only difficult for her because she was dealing with a dead body, but because Captain Swain had taken Slater under his wing during training.

Ryan knew Swain had had a daughter. Often older soldiers parented younger soldiers, them becoming placeholders for actual family members. Ryan didn't even have kids and he did the same thing sometimes.

Ryan would have removed Swain's gear himself but commanders needed to delegate, no matter how much they wanted to take on every task.

And Bates didn't look like he was in any shape to take command, something he should have done already, being an officer.

But a soldier like Ryan was used to giving orders while officers, no matter their rank, pretended to be in charge and took credit for the success of a mission. True soldiers didn't wear a uniform for pats on the back.

Bates stared at the ground as if he could discover a way back to base under the dirt. Ryan thought about letting him keep it up but he needed to know the status of every soldier even if he outranked him.

"What's the status of your weapon, sir?"

"I don't have a head injury, Sergeant."

Act like it then.

Ryan observed that everyone—except Bates, Moss, and Tower—were now sitting, squatting, or leaning against debris. Parts of the A-brid might flame up again. Fire was every soldier's enemy.

"On your feet," Ryan commanded.

Let's prove we're fit to survive.

The squad acted like the command was the last thing they wanted to hear at first, but everyone not already standing, stood. Not fast enough for Ryan but he let it go. They were alive and seemed to be uninjured; bodily.

"Newlin," Ryan said, "front and center."

Newlin hustled in front of Ryan. "Sergeant?"

"Look at me." Ryan examined Newlin's pupils. "No sign of head injury. You good to go?"

"Good to go, Sergeant."

"Examine everyone else to make sure they are too."

"Yes, Sergeant."

When Newlin stood in front of Bates, Bates glared at him, ironically giving Newlin a better look at his eyes, so Newlin went to Slater.

"Dehydration is our enemy," Ryan said. "I want everyone sipping water. If anyone has symptoms of dehydration, I want to know about it. Understood?"

The squad replied, *"Yes, Sergeant."*

Except for Bates.

Ryan ignored Bates as he tried to think of anything else of importance. The weather was warm, they were far from the elevation of the mountains, so cold weather injuries weren't an immediate concern.

"Keep socks dry. We all understand the importance of hygiene given our situation."

What else?

"Gather everything useful that's intact. We need to know which weapons are fully mission capable and which ones are not. Hopefully all of them are. See how much water and how many MREs we have. And how much ammo. I want rucks packed with everything we need and then some. Understood?"

The squad replied, *"Yes, Sergeant."*

Bates said nothing.

"Tower," Ryan said, "what's the status of your gear?"

"One-hundred percent."

"Good. Guard the squad while we inventory our equipment and assess functionality."

"Yes, Sergeant."

Moss had already been examined by Newlin. "Sergeant Ryan, may I provide overwatch?"

"Negative," Ryan said. "Let's belay that option. I want the squad to stick together. We don't need any additional missions. No offense."

Moss smirked. "None taken, Sergeant."

Burbano gave Newlin a pat on the back as he went to examine Page for a head injury, and asked aloud what everyone was thinking. "So, what the hell happened?"

CHAPTER 9

What happened indeed.

Experienced soldiers dealt in contingencies. A mission getting fouled up was practically expected, but a crash that wasn't the result of pilot error, or faulty equipment, was quite different. Something alive was the cause.

Mission pressure could knock focus out of alignment and even to slowly erode, so Ryan would keep an eye on the squad and ignore who he suspected the weakest link to be, until he proved it to be true.

If Bates was the kind of person who focused under pressure, then all the better, and Ryan would never have to tell anyone. But he already had his suspicions about him, and fortunately they outnumbered him.

No doubt the pilot, McGary, felt responsible, even though he shouldn't; it was an accident.

"McGary," Ryan said. "I'm sorry about the brid."

He nodded. "At least we have ammo."

McGary was right to think forward, displaying how many years he'd worn a uniform. Having plentiful ammunition was a definite plus in their situation. Loaded magazines stuffed LBVs.

Plenty of ammo was never enough though, especially considering they didn't know what to expect.

Which threats to expect.

Tuhrelevim had a lot of unidentified wildlife, and most of the planet was uncharted.

"And food," Slater said.

Enough meals for a week for each soldier with Swain dead. Everything carried by the captain had been parceled out. Each of them carried a stuffed rucksack.

The average soldier could live on one MRE a day, longer when parceled out, and something they would be disciplined about doing.

Tower was the biggest of them, weighed the most, so he would need the most calories per day. Most likely he'd refuse to eat his fill, and could do—they all could—as their survival training was a commonality.

"Shouldn't there be a bunch of animals running around?" Slater said. "It's like something scared them off."

"Do you think it might have been the A-brid plummeting from the sky?" Page asked her.

Slater's eyes narrowed, giving him a look.

"I'd bet we're in established territory," Moss said.

Ryan wouldn't take that bet. Every soldier scanned the terrain, as if fearing something might rear up out of nowhere. Ryan had to admit he feared the same thing.

"I remember a shadow," Burbano said. "A big one before we went down."

"Me too," Ryan said.

"I think maybe that's what caused us to crash."

"I think you're right."

"It must have been one of those predators, the ones McGary saw." Burbano looked to McGary.

"I'm not sure what I saw," McGary said. "Happened so fast. Like the nearest mountain was leaning toward us."

"Strange."

"I know. I've never experienced that in all my days as a pilot."

"Shadows," Page said. "Bloody shadows."

"What caused the crash was an accident," Bates stated, "nothing more."

"I don't believe so, sir," Burbano insisted. "It was a deliberate attack. Whatever it was, it hit us like a missile."

"That's an exaggeration." Bates sighed. "And no one counted on the explorers getting lost."

"What's that got to do with it?" Burbano cleared his throat

quickly. "What's that got to do with it, sir?"

"No one ever does is my point."

No one ever does what? Ryan wanted to ask Bates, and no doubt so did Burbano, and also everyone else in the squad, but Ryan shook his head. *Don't antagonize him.*

Burbano nodded. If Bates spouted incomprehensible things sometimes, they could live with it. As long as he was an effective officer.

"Anyone know any of them?" Page asked. "The explorers."

Ryan wasn't the only one who could read into what was going on. Page meant to help dissuade confrontation too, even though his rank was Private First Class.

"Meet any of them personally?"

"None of *us*." Burbano looked around. "Who I know of. Just their feats and admirable educations."

"Worth spit out here," Slater said, sounding less like a private and more like a specialist, or even a sergeant.

"Will we wait for a rescue?" Newlin asked.

"The soldiers who would rescue us haven't landed yet," Ryan said.

"Send out the first. Smart, right?"

Ryan grinned. "I know."

"No kidding, man," Burbano said. "Unbelievable."

"*As* I *said*," Bates said. "And we all knew the risk."

"No one's coming for us," Ryan said. "We're going to have to get ourselves out of here. You care to chime in about how we're going to do that, sir?"

Bates had been chatty, but now looked like he was about to vomit at the suggestion. "It doesn't matter what we do. It's going to end the same for all of us."

"That's a fine attitude, sir."

"Are you mocking me?"

"Of course not."

The snickering of Ryan's compatriots told otherwise, but Bates got hold of his military bearing. "We've been through a lot. I'll forgive any disrespect to me, to my rank, before now, but from now on, no longer, not from anyone. Is that understood?"

The squad replied, *"Yes, sir."*

Bates had been slouching, and he stood up straight. "I am in command."

"That's what we were waiting for, sir," Ryan said. "Welcome aboard."

"Careful, Sergeant."

Ryan felt a flare of anger. Ryan held the highest rank in the squad—who wasn't an officer—by being a staff sergeant, so he was comfortable pushing an officer when they needed it, but they were only a squad, and down a man with the captain dead.

Ryan must lead by example. If he disrespected the lieutenant—and he really wanted to continue testing him, to shape him into a true member of the squad—most likely others would too.

That wouldn't help them survive. They needed to act as a team. And their team included everyone.

Ryan would try to figure out another way to push Bates and mold him into the leader they needed him to be under the current circumstances. There wasn't the time for him to do it under ideal ones.

Sustaining respect to rank could be trying during missions, but as Ryan had done during the past, and many times before, he allowed his anger to dissolve and sputter to nothingness.

Ryan eyed the body of Swain. "Private Slater. Private Page."

"Yes, Sergeant?" they said.

"Work together and put Captain Swain in a body bag. If anyone has anything to say, in regards to him as a person or his military service, now would be the time."

"What is the plan, sir?"

Bates seemed to be thinking about that before Ryan even asked, and he replied, "Give me a moment."

They did. As they waited, they ignored that Bates was wasting daylight.

Finally, he spoke up. "Secure the perimeter."

"Where is the perimeter, sir?" Tower asked.

Bates swallowed, examining their surroundings, seeing what they all did; tall, craggy mountains far in the distance, with hills closer, and tall grass that looked to be growing everywhere and closing in on them.

The grass swayed constantly being so tall. Some blades looked to be over ten feet and on the verge of falling over. The grass seemed to grow anywhere there wasn't water.

"Approximately one-hundred meters in every direction." Bates's voice cracked. "Arm yourselves and move out."

They were holding loaded weapons already, and the Rovlas were nearly at the ready—everyone sensed the unknown surrounding them—but Ryan spoke up quickly to avoid disrespect that might lean toward an unnecessary confrontation.

"Understood, sir," he said. "You all heard him. Let's get it done. But don't enter the grass. Right, sir?"

"Correct, Sergeant."

"Leave rucks in place. One-hundred meters or allow ten meters from the grass."

Bates looked like he was about to object, but instead he wore his annoyed face, put a hand on the butt of his pistol in the holster, wrapped an arm around his Rovla, stared at the ground, and marched forward.

He'd chosen a sector without telling anyone where he was going, silently counting paces. Ryan received glances from his compatriots.

"I know our compasses are what they are but they're mostly in sync," Ryan said. "Burbano and Moss, north. Tower, south. The lieutenant is going east, so I'll go northeast. Page and Slater, west." Ryan eyed McGary.

The pilot outranked him, but Ryan sensed McGary was like all of them while working as a team. Outranked or not, a true soldier could simply fall in.

"McGary," Ryan said, "will you remain here?"

McGary didn't hesitate. "You got it."

"What about me, Sergeant?"

"Newlin, you're with me."

CHAPTER 10

"Sergeant Ryan!" Bates called out while staring at the crash site, "please assemble the men near what is left of the A-brid!"

They could all hear him, and Bates had grouped in Moss and Slater by saying men—Slater grinned at Ryan—but at least Bates was respecting rank and delegating, acting like he was in charge. Ryan appreciated it.

Maybe Bates has finally gotten his shit together.

After Bates's brief command to secure the perimeter, and him deciding that there was no danger, Ryan realized his doubts about Bates's leadership had especially degraded after he refused to say a word about Swain or even attend his brief memorial.

Bates seemed angry about Swain dying. There'd been no discussion about what to do with the body bag yet. But as long as Bates continued to lead going forward, Ryan could stifle what he really thought about the man.

Ryan didn't have to like a superior in order to obey his or her orders. "Back to the crash site! All of you!"

"I don't trust him, Sergeant," Newlin said.

Ryan felt the same way but he couldn't have the chain of command break down. They had enough problems. "You heard the lieutenant."

The soldiers hustled back to the crash site as ordered, and all of them seemed to be anxious for the next order.

Ryan was too. He wasn't sure what Bates had planned, but hopefully he was ready to move out.

If the body bag was to be carried along with them, as it should, then Tower would be carrying one side by the handle.

Let him do something with those muscles.

There were still cords of smoke rising into the air. The only thing that could have been done about it was covering them with dirt, but there were no more flames. The destruction seemed safe enough to linger.

"Attention, men. I am the perfect officer to lead this mission. I've had years of experience leading soldiers and many years of training. I want you all to have my back, and obey my every command as I lead the way forward."

Slater turned her head to laugh quietly, and Ryan felt the flood of apprehension. If Bates had commanded them to feel confused and nervous then it would have been mission accomplished.

Except Bates's career had gotten him this far. Ryan had been aware of him before deploying to Planet Tuhrelevim and heard nothing but positives around base other than him being a control freak; but so many who were in charge were.

Although Ryan had his doubts, he did his best to hide them. "What *is* the mission going forward, sir?"

"We are going to remain here and keep the perimeter secured."

"At the crash site?"

"At the crash site, sir."

"At the crash site—"

"Or we may leave soon. I don't know."

"You *need to know*, sir," Tower said.

Tower said it before Ryan did. Bates's view shifted up at Tower.

"Sergeant Tower is correct, sir."

Ryan had to concentrate on speaking to the lieutenant with as much respect as possible. It was the stress of the situation that was causing his military bearing to slip. Ryan almost said you need to have a definitive plan.

"We need to have a definitive plan."

Unfortunately, Bates could care less about Ryan's respect or logic. "I don't appreciate your disrespectful tone, Sergeant Tower. Apparently, all of those pushups while we were airborne did nothing for your senses."

Tower smirked and he seemed about to really dig into Bates.

"Tower," Ryan said, "go clean your weapon."

Tower hesitated.

"Sergeant Tower."

"Gladly."

Tower ejected the magazine, yanked the charging handle—catching the chambered round in the air—then tossed his Rovla up, grabbing it by the hand guard before marching away.

When Tower was out of earshot, Ryan motioned with his head, "Sir, a word?"

Bates looked ready to chase Tower down and tackle him, but instead he went along with Ryan.

Ryan made sure it was in the opposite direction of where Tower had gone.

Bates stared through Ryan, even while he spoke. "What will we do with Captain Swain's body?"

"He's dead. What is done with it is irrelevant."

"Sir?"

"Is there a problem?"

"What *will* be done with him?"

"Whatever you think is best."

"All right. Then wherever we go, we take him along with us."

"I've already decided we will remain here. Were you not paying attention?"

"I meant if anything changes, sir. Which you hinted at."

"Is that why you needed to speak with me? Something tells me you wouldn't be questioning every order by Captain Swain. If he were still alive."

"Orders are exactly what I need to hear and the specifics of them what I need to know."

"I'm in charge—"

"That's not in question. Sir, we need to be on the same page."

"We are on the same page."

"I don't feel that way."

"And why is it that you don't feel that way?"

"Because I don't know what's going on."

"Then ask."

"That is what I'm doing. That is my purpose right now. And it's also important for us to be on the same page in front of the squad. Although I trust your judgment," Ryan lied, "the current situation will continue to be challenging for all of us."

"Pages of a book can be torn or burned to a crisp until there is nothing at all. Tell me something I don't know already. Were you not *listening* to my orders?"

Again, Ryan felt his temper pulse, but, also, he had no idea what Bates was talking about. Ryan wondered if Bates was losing it. He heard of people losing their minds after going to a different planet.

Bates might be Ryan's first encounter with such madness, and hopefully the last.

"Remaining here, sir? Or moving out?"

Bates took a step toward him. They were nearly nose to nose. Maybe it was Ryan who Bates wanted to fight all along.

Maybe Ryan knew that deep down and that was why he'd asked to speak with him alone.

Bates was slightly taller than Ryan, but Ryan had him by roughly twenty pounds. He thought he could take him.

There were always seconds leading up to a physical altercation, recognizable if it had happened before.

Preventable or a go.

It seems to be a go.

But instead of becoming more aggressive, Bates backed away, seemingly aware of what was about to happen, no doubt sensing it from Ryan.

Ryan was relieved. It would be quite the contradiction ordering the squad to respect Bates only for Ryan to knock him on his ass.

"You've got a lot of nerve questioning my orders, Sergeant."

"I'm not questioning you, sir," Ryan lied. "I'm just trying to get some clarification."

Bates reacted as if he'd been slapped. "Excuse me?"

Fuck it.

Ryan had had enough. "Time for you to man up, sir. You're in charge. I get that. But I need a definitive order to command the squad. We can't all be thinking we're doing different things. It's dangerous. I'm sure you understand."

"Then pay attention. What I say goes. That was one of my original orders. Or do I need to strip you of rank and make someone else my second in command?"

Ryan not only wanted to fight Bates, he wanted to tear him in half, but the distance between them was helping him control himself.

It was clear that the lieutenant had no idea what he was doing, or what he wanted to do. He seemed to be panicking, but confronting him about it might make things worse.

Until Ryan figured out a better way to get everyone back to base safely, and alive, he would fall in without question.

"Sergeant Ryan! Did you not hear me? Do you need to be punished?"

Bates's shouting drew attention, distracting the squad from their priority of guarding a perimeter that seemed impossible to secure, per Bates's command.

That included Moss, who looked ready to back Ryan up by giving him a knowing look. But he shook her off, focusing again on Bates. Bates looked over quickly but hadn't seen it.

"Of course not, sir," Ryan said, flexing calmness. "I apologize for any disrespect. Going forward, my attention to detail will be flawless."

"Make sure of it," Bates spat, turned, and marched back toward the group.

But endanger my soldiers unnecessarily and see what happens.

CHAPTER 11

"Whatever it was," Burbano said, "the rotor sliced it up."

"Mostly mist," Slater said.

They examined the fleshy remains. There was blood too, dark and dried from the sun where it sprayed. Patches of it glistened.

Burbano had been determined to prove Bates wrong, that it wasn't just some random accident, and had turned over damaged parts of the A-brid until he discovered the evidence he sought.

It was difficult to tell what the thing had been. From what there was, there were only small pieces. But it had definitely been an animal.

"Could it have jumped by accident?" Page asked.

"No way." Tower's weapon shined as if it were brand new. He knocked the magazine against his helmet to seat the rounds and slapped it into the magazine well. "It was the cause, like you said, Burbano."

"We need to hump it back to base," Burbano said.

"About a thousand klicks." Tower yanked the charging handle, loading the first round into the chamber of the Rovla. "I'm good with that. Too easy."

"What else are we going to do?" Newlin asked rhetorically. "Comms are zilch."

Slater looked around. "If you guys are right, there's obviously something out there that doesn't like us very much."

"It's going to be night soon." Bates closed his eyes and snapped them open. "We will play to the winds and decide, I will decide, what to do next but I will wait until it is morning."

Burbano mouthed, "*The fuck*?"

"We're going to remain here all night?" Ryan asked. "Are you sure that's wise, sir?"

"That's what I said, Sergeant. Do you believe it's wise to march during the dark? I need to get some rest." Bates coughed without covering his mouth. "I trust all of you will guard me."

They could use the rest.

"Others can rest at the same time, sir," Ryan said. "Good idea."

Before Bates could sound off with any attitude, Ryan ordered Moss, Slater, Page, and Newlin to go down.

When Slater asked where, he commanded her to dig a foxhole wherever was best. Moss was already holding her e-tool.

Digging a foxhole must not have occurred to Bates, and again Ryan got the feeling he wasn't right in the head, but still he followed Moss's lead and grabbed the e-tool off of his rucksack, chose a spot, and began digging.

The others started digging a distance away from where Bates did. Ryan gave the others a look that meant they would talk soon, once Bates was asleep. Or pretending to be asleep.

Ryan trusted Bates less and less.

Burbano shook his head. "Seriously, *what* in the *hell*?"

"Well said," McGary agreed.

"This guy is in charge?" Burbano said. "Man, I wish the captain was still . . ."

Ryan glared at him.

"I mean I wish Swain was still alive for himself of course, shitty that he died, but also for us. We could trust *him*. I don't trust this guy at all. I wish it had been . . ."

"Don't say it," Ryan said. "We don't need that."

Burbano exhaled. "I know, I know."

Ryan, McGary, and Burbano stood in a close circle facing outward, nearly back-to-back. That way they could speak frankly, quietly, and also keep an eye on the surroundings.

Tower stood guard over everyone else who were getting rest a distance away.

Not even Tower had been sure what he was guarding them

from, but everyone remembered the packs of predators McGary had seen while they were airborne, and the shadow before the crash.

It was impossible not to sense the wildlife on the planet. And hear it. The bugs were constant. And wherever there was wildlife, some of them were predators.

Ryan glanced over. Bates had rolled onto his side in the foxhole and seemed to be asleep.

Moss was dutifully asleep.

Newlin, Page, and Slater were still awake, probably whispering and irritating Tower.

Ryan could see Tower mouthing something, no doubt threatening to sleep in one of their foxholes if they didn't try and get some shuteye. It's what Ryan would have said to them.

"Here's what I'm saying, Sergeant," Burbano said, "and I'm sure I'm not alone about this, is that we go along with him, but when it comes down to it—"

"OK, OK," Ryan said. "I gotcha. I know. I give the real commands, I agree. We're going to survive this. The leaning cliffs of Fort Beckett will be in view before we know it."

Ryan tried his best to say it with as much conviction as he could, but even he didn't feel that way. They all must have sensed how much danger they were in. They didn't respond.

"You guys hear me?"

"I hope so, Sergeant," Burbano said. "But so far from base, limited weapons and supplies, and only so much ammo. If the unknown converges on our location—"

Ryan was thinking the same thing. "Enough of that. What did I just say?"

Burbano forced a smile. "Understood. I'm sure you've learned I'm the type who just needs to vent once in a while. Get it out, you know? When it comes down to it, I'm good to go."

"From now on, keep that shit to yourself."

"Yes, Sergeant."

"Yeah, Burbano," McGary said. "Quit being paranoid, you're scaring me."

Burbano socked his shoulder, "That's for scaring *us* on the A-brid."

McGary rubbed his shoulder. "Ow."

Burbano gave him a look.

Ryan said, "McGary, you got anything?"

"Negative."

Ryan pulled his Rovla close to his chest, the barrel angled and aiming at the ground. "Both of you go get some sleep. Tell Tower too. I'll assume guard duty."

"That's good of you, Sergeant," Burbano said. "I'll sleep for what, a few hours?"

"Yes."

"Thank you. I need it. Then you can take my foxhole"

Ryan nodded and took on his responsibility.

CHAPTER 12

"I'm telling you I saw something."

It was Slater's voice. Panicked. Undisciplined. Closer to civilian than soldier because of her rank of private.

Often soldiers with higher rank felt the same way Slater did, all of that training coming undone, but commanding soldiers of lower rank belayed expressing it until it could be ignored altogether.

So much stress could be dissolved by focusing on helping others.

One of the benefits of being around soldiers of lower rank was honesty. It was difficult to know what was really going on from a soldier like Tower; his blood type was stoicism.

Halfway through the night, it had been Ryan's turn to rest. Fortunately, foxholes had been dug already. Another benefit of having a higher rank than the others. The ground never ideal for sleeping, extra clothing suited as a field pillow just fine.

Ryan was on his feet, had grabbed his weapon, and had joined them. "Sitrep." He yawned.

"Why is it always the FNG who sees ghosts?" Page asked.

"Fuckin' new gal in my case. It was right there." Slater pointed at nothing.

Ryan inspected the grass, searching for any signs of life. Wind pushed grass forward and back and side to side as if all of it were alive.

Hundreds, thousands, of uncountable separate growths of different sizes blew around, and all of it reached toward them before leaning away again, then going in different directions.

Anything could be in there.

"What was it?" Ryan asked.

"Some kind of animal," Slater said.

"Explain."

"A shape. As we were talking, its head tilted to the side like it was listening. I stepped back. As I did, it sank out of view. I got everyone's attention. When I turned to look again, it was gone. I know I saw it. I know I saw something."

"A predator?"

"Definitely."

"Give me more details."

"I didn't see it clearly but it had a very muscular body for something on all fours. I think it was striped. Big teeth. A tail. I wish Nimbus was here."

"Not me," Page said. "Biologist or not, that guy gives me the creeps."

"I meant for his expertise," Slater said. "Give us some insight into what we're dealing with."

"From my experience, the best intel comes from those on the ground," Ryan said. "Nimbus is always in the TOC."

"Agreed I guess, Sergeant," Page said. "Slater, are you sure you weren't seeing things?"

Slater nodded. "Positive."

Ryan looked to Moss, their sniper. "Private?"

"I don't doubt Slater," Moss said. "But I missed it. I was still waking up."

"McGary," Ryan said, "did the animals beneath us on the A-brid have tails?"

"Negative."

"So, we're dealing with something new."

"Slater's telling the truth," Tower said.

Tower was about ten meters away with his weapon aimed.

"What is it?" Ryan asked.

"Come see for yourself."

"Remain staggered." Ryan hustled to where Tower was.

"See it?"

Ryan squinted. "I don't see anything."

"No, the ground."

Ryan looked down at the dirt and there was a four-toed paw-print. Claws had sunk into the soil showing how long and sharp they were.

"It looks like it was purposeful," Tower said. "Don't you think?"

Ryan didn't know what he meant. "Say again?"

"Look at the way it is."

Now Ryan saw it. "Like it's meant as a threat."

"Or it's messing with us. A tactic."

"Come on."

"Maybe a mark left for its own kind. Similar to marker flags explorers were supposed to place." Tower adjusted his chin strap. "There's something here. Right in there or close by."

Ryan adjusted his weapon. "If it was going to attack, why hasn't it?"

"That's the question."

"What was under the A-brid must not have lost interest in us as we'd hoped."

"Right. It can't be a coincidence."

"Even so, we shouldn't assume anything."

"What is happening?" It was Bates's voice.

"Shit," Tower whispered, "he's awake."

"Be careful about that."

"I have to or else I'm gonna knock his ass out. Don't worry, when it comes to whispering, I'm a sniper."

They had been willing to allow Bates to sleep as long as possible, so they wouldn't have to deal with him. It had been decided through telepathy.

Bates adjusted his uniform, straightening it. He'd left his flak jacket, helmet, rucksack, and weapon at the foxhole.

As calmly as Ryan could, he said, "You might want to remain armed and armored from this point on, sir."

"Then we all will. What's going on?"

They all wore full battle rattle and held weapons, but Ryan just pointed. "Something left that. To signal others of its species maybe."

"Finally."

"*Sir*?"

Bates smiled creepily and looked up at the night sky. "No one understands me."

Ryan saw Tower's free hand clench into a fist as they waited for what he would say next.

Bates had denied he'd gotten a head injury, and Ryan hadn't been sure about that, but now he believed him.

Although impressive in his determination, attentiveness, and assertiveness, Ryan had to admit that Bates had always given him the creeps. Before being assigned to the squad, and the mission, Ryan just hadn't heard him say that much.

Bates was simply very strange, and his behavior was being affected by the crash or by being on the new planet.

Bates clasped his hands behind his back. "Now I'm finally certain what the mission should be. Will be."

PART 2

Operation Iron Sights

CHAPTER 13

According to Bates, the mission was to guard the perimeter and remain there until they were rescued, even though it was already discussed.

The day flew by. Discussions happened, cryptically, away from the prying eyes and ears of the lieutenant.

"It just doesn't make sense," Tower whispered. "Same as before. It's a shit plan."

"It is," Ryan agreed.

"*Bates* isn't making any sense. He's all over the place. Goes back and forth all of the time. The likelihood of us being rescued is as certain as reliable comms being set up before we return to base on foot."

"He's in denial about the obvious."

"Worse than that, he's gonna get us killed."

"We won't allow that to happen."

"How? The longer we're out here . . . I understand the risk of this job and I love that about it, but I want to decide when to take off my uniform. Not let some officer prick decide for me, and permanently."

"We've been through it before."

"Not like this. This isn't outlaws or space bugs."

"If he suggests something that's too dangerous—"

"Like he is now?"

"When there are better options, I'll make suggestions."

"And if he doesn't go along with them?"

"Then I'll think of a way to make it his idea."

Tower nodded. "I don't like that grass at all."

Because the grass was so tall, even the slightest wind caused it to bow and wave and shake, and so much of it stirring together made it seem as if something large was moving around unseen.

"If there's an animal in there, it's using it as cover," Tower said. "I would. We should burn it all down."

"And signal our location to others?" Ryan said.

"Maybe one of ours might see it."

"That's a slim maybe. We don't know what else might be watching. Or how many of them."

Tower scratched at a stubbly chin that needed shaving. "Understood."

"Contact!"

McGary's warning was followed by gunfire exploding along the perimeter. It wasn't just one soldier firing, they all seemed to be, and Ryan and Tower hustled to join the rest of the squad.

Even Moss was shooting. Her sniper rifle was slung over her back and she fired Swain's Rovla in controlled bursts.

Ryan couldn't identify what they were shooting at. There was just grass as far as he could see. "Cease fire!"

The squad did as he commanded followed by a few additional discharges. Glances went at Ryan while they were ready to start shooting again.

Bates aimed a pistol, but it didn't seem he'd fired it, ignoring his slung Rovla. He looked like he'd seen a ghost.

"What are you shooting at?" Ryan asked. No one answered. "McGary, sitrep."

"What made the pawprint," McGary said. "I think."

"What you saw while piloting the A-brid?"

"I don't know. What Slater saw? It was so fast."

"Slater."

"I don't know, Sergeant."

"Did you see it?"

"Negative, Sergeant."

"Then why were you discharging your weapon? Why were you *all* shooting?"

Slater wiped her brow. "Following McGary's lead, Sergeant."

That made Ryan proud. *But the strength of our squad could be used against us.*

"Let's not forget our mission, locating fellow humans, nearby and trying to survive like we are."

"Do you really think—"

"I don't care what I think. Higher will determine the status of the explorers upon our return."

"Yes, Sergeant."

"In the future, if you choose a sector of fire, ensure you only shoot at an enemy. And you better put it down. Do you see a body?"

"No, Sergeant."

"Shell casings without a body is a no-go. Is that understood?"

"Yes, Sergeant."

"That's not just for Private Slater, obviously, that's for everyone. Let me hear it."

The squad replied, *"Yes, Sergeant."*

Except for Bates, who shook his head for some reason, looking up at the sky, then at the ground, shaking it some more.

Ryan knew better than to ask him what he was doing. Ryan was having trouble remembering one time when Bates responded and it made sense.

They waited for the threat to show itself again. Just because Ryan had ordered the squad to be disciplined about discharging their weapons, that didn't mean they weren't ready to squeeze triggers.

"Chief McGary," Ryan said. "What else do you recall about the creature?"

"It showed itself and then it was gone just as quick. But its face. Hatred, man. I could sense it."

"How would you feel about us if you were it?" Tower asked.

"Scared, I guess. Especially of you, Tower."

"We need to get our asses back to base," Burbano said. "Whatever it is, it doesn't want us here."

"Is that news?" Tower asked.

"You can't know what you're talking about, Sergeant Burbano," Bates told him.

"It's not like we want to stay, sir."

"I agree," McGary said. "We don't belong. Period."

"Chief McGary—"

"No, you don't have any authority over me, Bates! I'm the pilot, not an established member of the squad. If anyone should be giving orders, it's me not you."

"We abide by military laws from Earth."

"We haven't done that for decades."

"And what would Colonel Horne say to that?"

"Let's go ask him!"

"Maybe you should remain here with the remnants of your precious aircraft once we're rescued, pilot!"

"There won't be any rescue, you—"

"Men, enough!" Ryan said. "We gotta focus on solving the obstacles of the here and now."

It was as if Ryan had been witnessing the military as he knew it coming undone forever. He envied the soldiers on Earth centuries ago. So many concrete laws and hundreds of years of established repeated customs.

But out in space?

Soldiers out there were barely hanging on to what was. Ryan wouldn't be surprised if the traditional military—wearing uniforms and understanding and respecting rank and all of it—disappeared forever.

McGary trusted Ryan, he knew, and had subtly conceded to his decisions, but he wasn't about to do that with Bates.

With Captain Swain dead, for the first time during his career, Ryan didn't know who should actually be in charge according to rank; McGary or Bates?

Ryan probably wasn't the only one who was confused, Bates and McGary obviously didn't know either, and that was probably why Bates was so angry.

None of them had experienced a mission going south in such a way before. Especially on an alien planet.

Ryan kept hearing something or it was his imagination, but he was leaning toward the former.

The tips of grass were an ocean to conceal sounds, obscuring what was happening beneath. Whatever it was in there, it was probably as comfortable as an aquatic animal to the sea.

Something muffled, like pressure against the greenery. Quiet and steady within all of those long, skinny bayonet shapes, green and flitting around endlessly.

Careful steps of paws?

Ryan knew to display confidence if that were the case, to fake it if necessary, even to a beast.

And if it was really there, Ryan remembered learning something else important about predators, and how they viewed prey facing away from them.

"No one turn their back to the grass."

"Yes, Sergeant."

CHAPTER 14

"No comms," Newlin said. "No artillery if we need it."

"Artillery," Burbano said, "are you kidding me?"

"I don't know, it just occurred to me, Sergeant. Nothing secures a perimeter better than steel rain."

"True, but it would be a danger close cluster f—forget that. I'll take my chances with a weapon in hand."

"Then we stand our ground," Bates said.

Ryan and Bates were in agreement on that much. For now. It was almost night again.

Already.

"Sir," Moss said. She had unblended from the background. "Since we're going to remain here for the foreseeable future, permission to hike the nearest ridge to provide overwatch?"

Ryan smirked, and Moss smirked back at him with her eyes. She obviously disagreed with Ryan when he'd rejected the suggestion earlier.

Her face had remained painted and as camouflaged as her uniform. All positives for a sniper, he supposed. But it couldn't hide how pretty she was.

Bates nodded as if it were his idea. "Granted. Go."

Moss handed Tower the Rovla. "Hold on to this for me, Sergeant?"

"Don't be gone too long."

"Yes, Sergeant."

No matter how he felt about Moss, Ryan thought it was a bad idea to separate. "Sir . . . Shouldn't we stick together?"

"I said *go*," Bates said to Moss.

"It's OK, Sergeant Ryan," Moss said. "This is what I do best." She started running for the ridge. “Trust me!”

Ryan reminded himself that a sniper was the pulse of war, and if one of them saw the need to take action, the rest of the soldiers were wise to follow their lead.

“Look at it this way, Sergeant,” Bates said. “She may prompt the beast to appear.”

“None of my soldiers are expendable, sir. Especially, to use as bait.”

“It seems you didn’t read the fine print on your enlistment papers.” Bates activated his shoulder radio. “Moss, are you in position? Over.”

Fuck you, Bates.

“Private Moss. I say again, are you in position? Over.”

Moss hadn’t responded.

“Give her a few minutes, sir,” Ryan said.

Bates sighed, annoyed. “I would be up there by now.”

Ryan shook his head, ending early the snickering that was about to start up from the rest of the soldiers.

Ryan—and the rest of the squad—would have *loved* to have seen who could get there first from the same starting position. They all remembered doing physical training together.

After seeing Moss run past him during a PT test, Ryan would bet his pension on her.

Bates huffed. “Private Moss, I say again, are you in *position*? *Over.*”

“Affirmative, over.”

Ryan exhaled a breath he didn’t realize he’d been holding.

“It’s about time, Private,” Bates said. “Situation report? Over.”

“Will you confirm my location?”

A shiny spot winked from the ridge. The scope on her sniper rifle.

“We see you. Sitrep? Over.”

“No target in sight. But I’ve discovered something. A helmet. Not ours, over.”

“Not ours? Explain, over.”

“Worn by a human pilot, but hundreds of years old by the look of it.

From the deep space explorers. From way back then I would guess. And it seems to be . . . it's been . . . admired, over."

"Say again? Over."

"There are pawprints around the base of it as if it was placed here to view. Very strange, break . . . Sir, squad, be very still. All of you. It just rose into view, over."

Ryan looked where he guessed Moss was viewing through her scope but saw nothing but grass. He looked to his compatriots but they didn't react either.

Bates twisted to the ridge in the distance and then back. "I don't see anything, over."

"It's right in front of you. About to pounce. Can't you see? Over."

Bates squinted, and then ricocheted glances around the squad. "Negative. Should we fire?"

An officer asking a private for permission to fire? And where?

"No, sir," Ryan said. No doubt Moss was thinking what Ryan did, that blindly firing their weapons again was a bad idea too, and she was watching them closely. "We should only expend ammo at a known target—"

"*I* was speaking to *Moss*, Sergeant Ryan." Bates activated his radio. "Private Moss, can you take the shot? Over."

"Affirmative, over."

"Take the shot."

"Wilco. Standby."

They waited . . . but there was no gunshot.

"It's on the move . . . It disappeared . . . No, I see it again. It's coming for me."

Strange, Ryan thought. They heard nothing, saw nothing. Ryan tilted his head and activated his shoulder radio. "Moss, do you refer to what was at our position? Over."

"Yes. Shit, it's fast."

"Shoot it," Bates commanded. "Private Moss?"

"It's avoiding my scope—switching to iron sights—give me cover fire —"

Seconds later there was a shot from the powerful Rovla sniper rifle, but the echo of the gunshot sounded away from them.

Ryan activated his shoulder radio. "Moss . . . Moss!" He turned toward the ridge. "I'm going after her."

"Do you need backup, Sergeant?" McGary asked.

"Negative."

"Sergeant Ryan," Bates said. "I have not given you permission to do so."

"Sergeant Tower will be your second in command until I return. If I give the command, give me cover fire."

Bates said something else but Ryan hadn't heard him, as he was already running. He went the same path as Moss did but approximately twenty meters east—if where she'd gone was designated north—and all of the way up the ridge.

By the time Ryan reached the top, he was winded. There was no sign of the threat Moss had described, or the helmet or pawprints. Instead there looked to be hurried scrape marks in the dirt, likely by claws.

It must have seen her up here and didn't like her messing with its treasure.

There was the same grass on the ridge up there as there was below, and it looked like something had lied down because it was flattened, and it didn't seem to be only from Moss lying down in the prone position.

Based on the blood there'd been a fight, but there was no sign of Moss's body, her sniper rifle, or what had done it.

Moss had to be around there somewhere, so he searched.

There was no sign of Moss beyond the blood. She'd been dragged into the grass and then she disappeared. Ryan could only explore so far. She could be alive, Ryan hoped, but he doubted it. It was a gut punch.

Moss had been an exceptional soldier, aside from ignoring a few direct orders. Ryan respected her, and personally, he had liked her.

Maybe a little too much.

He had definitely been attracted to her and there was a part of him that believed they might become a couple. He had no idea if the attraction was mutual. But whatever future there was between them had vanished with her disappearance.

If she wasn't killed, then she was taken somewhere. But where and for what purpose? If it was as bad as Ryan feared, then her fate was the same as the explorers they'd been sent out to search for, or worse. There was no time for grief.

Ryan had even returned to where Moss had been positioned on the ridge and slowly aimed his weapon in every direction, searching for the animal that did it, the last leg of the search and rescue mission for her that he'd assigned to himself.

"Sergeant Ryan, over," Bates said.

Moss wasn't supposed to go up here. Wasn't supposed to see what she saw.

And now Ryan was standing in the same place. It was the first time in a long time he actually felt the tangible stabs of fear. But also, he'd been correct. They shouldn't have separated.

"Sergeant Ryan. What is your status? Over."

Ryan activated his radio. "Private Moss . . . she has disappeared. Most likely killed in action, over."

"Are you positive? Over."

"There's blood and no sign of her, over."

"Do you have eyes on what did it? Over."

"Negative. Descending back to your location. How copy, over?"

"Good copy, over."

As Ryan returned to the squad, they seemed to hope he was mistaken somehow, and that Moss would appear.

"We don't separate again until we return to base," Ryan said. "You good with that, sir?"

Bates looked frozen for a moment longer, but reluctantly nodded. Tower slung the Rovla that had been carried by Swain before Moss had.

CHAPTER 15

It was impossible to identify who yelled in the dark, but based on the snarling, it sounded like someone was being torn apart by a pack of beasts.

Ryan wished he wasn't human and didn't have to sleep at all. That way, he could guard everyone every minute until they got back to base.

The confusion sent everyone running in the same direction. It was difficult to determine where that was at first. The struggle was everywhere, amplified by the nearby hills.

As if a tactic.

Someone had started a small fire to remain warm. Ryan hadn't agreed to that so it must have been approved by Bates or built by Bates himself.

The firelight messed with his night vision so it was difficult not to trip over something on the way. They should have completely cleared the area of debris after Bates decided they would stay.

The sounds were awful and whoever was being attacked was being shook around. There was screaming, then groaning.

Gunfire was intermittent, like his squad mates were taking turns, but Ryan heard the controlled bursts. No one wanted to take the time to reload.

The fire had hindered his vision, and was also hindered by the muzzle flashes of weapons shooting in the same direction.

Panicked voices and shouting bled through the lapses in gunfire. The gunfire turned undisciplined, sounding unlike how the soldiers of Iron Sights Squad typically fired weapons.

They'd shot thousands of rounds together while training, short controlled bursts all of them. A controlled burst was an impressive discipline, sounding like quickened falls of a hammer.

The way they were shooting now were like rounds going off by accident, and at random, triggers pulled—not squeezed—for too long. But Ryan understood why. He caught sight of it after the body was flung.

Just as he arrived, he saw shiny, bloody teeth followed by a tail as it turned, and then the rising shape dodged into the grass with a grumble and disappeared.

Ryan aimed . . . but didn't squeeze the trigger.

It will be back. We have only so much ammo.

Tower dragged Slater's corpse toward the smoking, makeshift fire-pit. It was still dark but the horizon was lightening. The sun would be up soon.

"Who the hell started that fire?" Ryan asked.

"I did," Bates said. "Who was watching her?"

"She went to urinate, sir," Newlin said.

"After what happened to Moss. You should have gone along with her, *Specialist*."

"She was in sight but I wanted to respect her privacy."

"You weren't guarding her closely enough."

"I know that, sir."

"It's no one's fault," Ryan said. "It wasn't your fault, Newlin."

Newlin nodded, and Ryan's voice seemed to calm everyone down. Long enough for even Ryan to feel some control over what had just happened.

"Two females in the squad and it's killed them both," Burbano said. "Why? Why them? It can't be a coincidence, right?"

No one had an answer, but all of them were likely busily trying to figure it out, and how much the deaths of Moss and Slater had weakened the squad. It was disturbing.

"Existence for most species revolves around its females," Ryan said. "If all of us had to die, save two, who would we want to survive? Who would we choose?"

"That is fucked up," Burbano said. "That thing *fucked* up. We're going to kill it."

"Damn right we are," Ryan said. "But it wants us angry, so we'll make mistakes." Ryan was shaken up by the discovery. The intelligence that it required. "We need to deal with it and with a purpose. Standing idly by is—"

"Armor that gallops," Bates said.

"Say again, sir?"

For a moment Bates seemed to have a secret, as if he'd discovered a spare and intact A-brid in his back pocket that was ready to fly them back to base and to safety, except he was only concerned for his own well-being and would be the only one on board.

Bates's features dissolved into his normally stern expression. "I saw nothing."

"That's not what I . . . Never mind."

"You sure about that, sir?" Tower asked.

Bates's helmet swiveled to lock on Tower. "Am I sure about what?"

"That you saw nothing. Or that you did nothing?"

Bates lunged, reaching up and grabbing the collar of Tower's uniform beneath his stubbly chin.

It was an odd sight someone so small confront Tower. Bates practically looked like a child next to him. Tower probably outweighed him by fifty pounds, and laughed at first.

Then he got angry. "Get your hands off me, sir."

"You were inferring something, were you not?"

"I infer nothing. I know you saw it but did nothing to warn us. You say anything different, then you're lying."

"I'm a liar, is that it?"

Tower's large hands closed over Bates's, dwarfing them, and he began prying them away from his person. "As I said."

Bates actually struggled against Tower's grip.

"Sir," Ryan said, "what are you doing?"

Tower flashed a glance at Ryan, silently asking permission, but Ryan shook his head. The men crowded around, sensing the fight, but it was already happening.

The thing was, it didn't go the way anyone thought it would.

Most of all Tower.

Bates was shorter than Tower—everyone was—but Tower's strength was used against him when Bates grabbed hold of a wrist and stepped away with a violent, sudden arc of his arms.

The momentum flipped Tower to the ground, and when he rolled, his legs landed like chopped down trees.

"You son of a bitch!" Tower yelled.

Bates fell on top of him, shoving Tower's own arm across his neck, and leaned against it while straddling him. Bates was pressing Tower's bicep into his own windpipe and using his helmet for grip.

"Call me a liar again!"

Tower's eyelids fluttered, about to lose consciousness.

"Sir, stop!" Ryan yelled.

Bates didn't react. He didn't stop. He didn't even flinch. In fact, he seemed to be determined not only to make Tower unconscious but to kill him.

Ryan rammed into Bates's armor with his shoulder, and Bates rolled off of Tower, but pulled him with him.

It was enough for Tower to take a breath as Ryan went sprawling. Tower grabbed LBV, yanked, and sent a hook into Bates's ribs, stunning him, allowing Tower the time to get to his feet.

Bates groaned and coughed, clenching fists at his sides as he stood. He was furious and ran at Tower again.

Tower was defensive, backing away, realizing he was outmatched hand to hand, pushing against Bates whenever he got near him.

Tower had to shove him away multiple times. Luckily neither man had used a weapon.

"Sir," Ryan said, "this isn't the place or the time."

"No kidding," Tower said. "We've got real problems."

"Sir," Ryan said. "Get a hold of yourself."

It was a silly thing to say after what happened, but it was the only thing Ryan could think of. His priority was not to antagonize Bates more. Another member of the squad had just died, and whatever did it was still out there.

We don't need two enemies!

Glancing around, Ryan saw the rest of the squad guarded them by aiming weapons outward.

"All of you have turned against me," Bates snapped. "And there will be consequences."

They all seemed to come to the same conclusion at the same time. Higher rank or not, they couldn't have an additional threat if they could help it. They wouldn't. They couldn't.

"Immobilize the lieutenant," Ryan commanded.

Bates scowled. "Don't you dare."

Ryan held a hand up, as if it could stop a bullet. "Drop your weapon, sir."

CHAPTER 16

Ryan had had enough of how dangerous Bates had become. And he knew the rest of the squad had too. It was a difficult command but he'd just reacted, and the rest of the squad backed him.

Insubordinate or not, Bates endangers the squad.

Bates was impressive at hand to hand combat, but not after everyone rushed him. Although it was more difficult fighting hand to hand wearing full battle rattle, they'd trained for that too.

Ryan felt sorry for the first soldier he got a hold of, Newlin, who yelled in pain after getting Bates to drop his pistol, his arm close to snapping, but blows to Bates's side and legs and shoulders relented his grip over him.

Bates went quiet as they subdued him, and once he was immobile, Ryan zip-tied his hands behind his back. He rolled him into a sitting position, and Bates sat on the ground like a defiant child.

Ryan couldn't believe he'd needed to do that. It was the first time he'd zip-tied anybody in his own squad outside training.

"What you have done is not only mutinous, but it's also—"

Burbano threw a bandana across his mouth and tied it to the back of his neck below his helmet. Then he knocked his knuckles against the top of it. "Let's not forget you were going to shoot one of us."

Bates argued against the bandana.

"Save your strength, Bates. You're going to need it," McGary said. "Sergeant Ryan, you are in command."

McGary flipped Bates off, and Bates mumbled, likely saying what McGary's finger meant.

Ryan appreciated the confidence coming from a warrant officer and nodded, looking around at his fellow soldiers, his squad.

"We're returning to base," he said. "We're going home."

"Finally, a command I can get behind," Burbano said. "We're in no shape to save anyone. If the explorers are out here somewhere . . . we don't know where."

"I agree," Ryan said. "We have water and MREs and our weapons. Extra clothing and more in our rucks. We don't need comms we have each other and our boots. We'll push it, but we'll rest when we need to, and we can purify any water source. Too easy."

"What if we run out of MREs?" Page asked.

"We eat what's edible. And I'll be the one to test whether anything other than meat is poisonous. If it comes to that."

Most animals could be eaten once cooked, they knew, but if it was anything else that might be edible, then the standard contact and taste tests applied.

They were on an alien planet, so it was probable not all definitive rules of nature—to human understanding, and from Earth—applied there. But maybe they did. Some of it did. They just didn't know if it was planet wide.

They would be on the lookout for the edibles that weren't fit for human consumption, what to avoid because people had tried them and died.

First round in the chamber.

Ryan didn't have to explain. His fellow soldiers had the same training. Perhaps as they got closer to Fort Beckett there would be comms. He didn't have to mention that part either.

"Ready yourselves."

With the imminent threat of the unknown lurking out there somewhere, the same that had been done with Captain Swain was done for Private Slater; her remains placed in a body bag and brief words said. While Ryan and Tower guarded them.

We can't bring along Moss's body because it's missing, but we'll damn well bring along Swain's and Slater's.

After, attention went to the swirling grass and the whereabouts of what dwelt within. The warmth of morning and a new day was of little consolation.

CHAPTER 17

They had condensed necessary supplies, loaded magazines, reloaded weapons, and even brought along a laser torch. Food and water were essential and everyone had as much as possible packed into their rucksacks.

They were bringing along everything they had of need for the trek back to base, and had even put the extra weapons inside Slater's body bag.

Ryan chugged cold coffee from a canteen cup. Tower thought it was a good idea and did the same.

McGary took the bandana off of Bates's mouth and tilted one of Bates's own canteens long enough for him to remain hydrated. But he placed and tied the bandana back on right afterward, not giving him enough time to swear.

Heading in the correct direction wouldn't be an issue. They had maps and were all experienced at land navigation. Because they were on an alien planet, some of them even took to studying those maps outside mission briefings, even trying to memorize them.

The potential obstacles would be bodies of water, hills, mountains, and the unknown.

But one obstacle at a time.

They had a long way to go, but they didn't have a choice. And they couldn't very well continue the mission. Doing so would have been suicide, likely adding *them* to the missing explorers, and would have meant an additional rescue mission.

Ryan would not allow that to happen. Their mission failing was his call.

They had ammo but only so much of it left, so Ryan concealed a sharp edge from the A-brid, wrapping the crude handle with tape.

He didn't know if he would need it but if he did he'd be glad to have it. He was embarrassed to admit he'd misplaced his combat knife after the crash. He had no idea where it was or what happened to it.

Captain Swain and Private Slater hadn't carried a knife, so it wasn't as if he could retrieve one from them after they'd died. Moss carried one, but she'd disappeared. A blade was always useful, no matter the condition, even if it was makeshift.

Tower had slung his Rovla assault rifle, it dangled at his front, and he carried the body bag with Captain Swain inside it over his shoulder, using his rucksack like a tabletop.

Newlin and Page carried the other body bag with Slater in it, each grasping an end by the handle.

McGary kept guard over Bates. He would remain gagged. Because it was up to Ryan, that bandana would remain over his mouth until they reached Fort Beckett. The exception would be whenever he ate or drank.

At least they no longer were dealing with Bates's lunacy. Ryan had no doubt extreme stress was affecting him. Ryan never had a problem with Bates before. But then again they'd never been on a real mission together either.

The path was easy enough to follow and they were careful to avoid what enveloped them, keeping their distance from the growths of green as much as possible.

The grass didn't grow everywhere but it grew thickly enough that it looked like a forest when standing before it. The forest of grass looked as if it would never end.

Ryan would bet it looked that way from the air too. He sure wished they could have flown home rather than walk.

Maybe they'd get lucky and stumble upon some communication equipment with stronger reception than what they had on their shoulders, or even a vehicle of some sort. But it was a safer bet to assume not. Explorers hadn't set out with much equipment either.

Every piece of equipment they would ever need existed, but the impatience of human beings caused the priority to explore first, then make a list of everything that was necessary, later.

It was mostly people who'd arrived on Tuhrelevim so far. Plentiful supplies and weapons were incoming; they'd been told.

Motivation was the only reliable resource, especially when low of options or out of them. The hard road was typically the surest way to reach a destination point, but when expected, that knowledge could be used as fuel.

Determination could be a fire burning, and extinguished only once a mission was complete.

For them, the new mission was to go home. And for soldiers, where they were stationed at was often home enough.

Better to remain a pessimist, and that nothing would go according to plan, but Ryan would be on the lookout for any unexpected tools of use, be it weapons, radios, or even vehicles.

Any of it might be possible to find. Unlikely, but he'd been pleasantly surprised before.

"Sergeant Ryan?"

Ryan called ahead to McGary. "Yes?"

"Bates has to urinate."

"Tell him he can hold it."

"I have to go too, Sergeant," Page said.

Tower turned with the body bag over his shoulder. "I could use the rest."

"Halt!" The soldiers did as Ryan commanded. "For those on guard, keep weapons aimed. McGary, ensure the lieutenant doesn't do anything stupid."

"Anything else stupid you mean."

Bates glared, his mouth moving, no doubt talking back, but as long as no one could understand him, they could ignore him.

CHAPTER 18

"McGary," Ryan said, "not so close. Back him up."

Bates had led McGary almost directly in front of the grass.

Too close.

McGary grabbed his LBV and towed Bates backward and then cut the zip-tie, freeing his hands. "Run and you get a bullet in the leg."

Turned out everyone needed to relieve themselves, Ryan included.

"Maybe this will show whatever's out there whose territory it really is," Burbano called out as he relieved himself.

"Not so loud," Ryan said.

"Yes, Sergeant. Just trying to . . . well, you know what I'm trying to do."

"I do." Ryan zipped up. "That doesn't mean it'll work."

"Yes, Sergeant."

When Bates was done, he'd obviously been holding it for a while, McGary secured his wrists again, this time in front of him, to give his shoulders a rest, and he seemed to appreciate it.

"Everybody good?" Ryan asked. The soldiers nodded. "Anybody need to squat over a hole?"

"I think I took care of that during the crash," Newlin said.

Others laughed quietly. Ryan tightened his grip on his weapon. The body bags were hefted up and once again they marched.

Burbano slowed, aiming his weapon. "Hear it?"

Tower twisted, holding the body bag over one shoulder and raising his strapped Rovla with his free hand. "Where?"

"Directly in front of us. Right in there."

The men went still, and remained silent. There was no use asking obvious questions. The truth would be revealed soon enough.

Ryan hoped Burbano was only being paranoid. They all aimed at the swaying strands of swirling anyway.

The strong wind was not helping. The grass itself looked alive, an unending ocean of churning growths of green.

"There could be anything in there," Burbano said. "Whatever killed Moss and Slater, I think it's following us."

"It probably didn't like us urinating," Page said.

"Move out," Ryan said.

"Sergeant Ryan," Page said, "may I speak with you?"

"We gotta stay with the group. We keep walking. What's on your mind?"

"I'm frustrated, Sergeant."

Everyone could hear Page as they were staggered only a few meters, but no one teased him.

"What's frustrating you?"

"All our training. How to defeat an enemy. It doesn't really apply to animals. We're the first round in the chamber, so our deceased captain conveniently declined night vision, but that would sure assist us at the moment."

"We can't change the past."

"How about our future?"

"In what way?"

"Our maps are dependable enough, but our compasses aren't completely reliable, they tend to be off, no one knows why. I mean they know why, but they haven't fixed it."

"Yet."

"Yeah, but until the updated models arrive—"

Ryan raised a hand. "I get it. But take away every weapon or piece of equipment from a soldier and he or she is still a soldier. Does that make sense?"

"Yes, Sergeant."

"Anything else, Private?"

"No, Sergeant."

Ryan actually agreed with Page as they walked side by side, there was a lot that could have been done before they lifted off for the mission with further preparation.

More equipment could have been issued that might have allowed them to finish the mission, more ammo and different weapon systems, to allow them to get back to base sooner.

But acknowledging that wouldn't help anything or anyone, so Ryan chose to stay motivated.

Even as shapes morphed from memories of vaguely familiar nightmares right in front of him and to the sides, as they kept on.

There were faces in the grass until they turned back to normal with flips by the wind, and there was whistling so loud that if there were steps by an animal then they wouldn't be heard at all.

"We really should burn it down," Tower said.

Silence was agreement.

But Ryan was in command. "I still think it's too risky."

"Now you sound like *you know who*," Tower said.

Bates swore through the gag.

"I agree with Sergeant Ryan," Newlin said.

"Me too," Page said.

"No, let's even the playing field," Burbano said. "If there isn't any grass to hide in, we'll be able to see it, so we can kill it."

"I'm sure you've noticed how much of it there is," Ryan said. "And do you really think it would remain near flames?"

"No, Sergeant, but—"

"No animal would. We'll keep the option on standby. Difficult controlling smoke. Even after fire burns out."

"Look, I'm not stupid. Obviously, we couldn't burn it all at once. I don't want to trap ourselves or burn ourselves up."

"We won't do it until the shit hits the fan."

"The shit *has* hit the fan, Sergeant. All respect."

"Deaths of our compatriots don't count as the shit hitting the fan?" Tower asked.

"Answer your own question, Tower," Ryan said. "What do you

think?"

"I think that most of us are alive."

"For now, we keep moving but we watch our six. Keep weapons at the ready."

The squad replied, *"Yes, Sergeant."*

CHAPTER 19

The beast was glimpsed when Tower got taken down. He dropped the body bag, and was dragged into the grass by his leg and out of sight. It happened so fast.

The uncharacteristic panic in Tower's voice already sounded a hundred meters away, and that he'd fallen down a cliff.

The soldiers reacted, and without thinking they all trampled into the unknown. Tower was hollering and his voice became even fainter. And then he sounded to be in extreme pain as they got closer.

Unfortunately, there was a blood trail to follow. McGary reached him first. Tower wasn't as far away as he'd sounded, the grass a natural silencer. He looked so small on the ground. Maybe it was because he was curled up in a ball and moaning.

"*Kill* the fucker. *Kill* it. Where the *fuck is* it? Kill it."

No one fired a weapon because there was nothing to shoot at. Except Ryan—and the rest of them—knew better.

"Keep weapons aimed and fingers on triggers," he ordered.

Ryan went to Tower and crouched. There was blood on his legs, and there were puncture wounds in the pant leg on one, but the wounds didn't seem as serious as Ryan expected.

Perhaps all of them rushing through the grass had scared it away? Ryan had his suspicions about the truth of that too.

"What's your status?" Ryan asked him.

Tower groaned. "What do you think?"

"Are you hurt or injured?"

Tower's next response was calmer. "I think both but I'll live."

"Can you stand?"

"Like I have a choice."

Ryan turned to his compatriots. “Help me.”

Burbano and Page slung their weapons and hustled over, carefully wedging themselves under Tower’s armpits, and with Ryan’s help—lifting from the front by gripping his LBV—Tower stood upright.

“Newlin,” Ryan said.

Newlin crouched, inspecting Tower’s leg. “Which one’s the most painful?”

“This one.” Tower gritted his teeth. “No tickling.”

Newlin smiled, dabbing at the wound with gauze. “It won’t require a tourniquet.”

“Cool,” Tower groaned. “Man, that thing is strong.”

“A surface bite, and it doesn’t look like any severe damage. There’s bleeding—”

“No shit.”

Newlin smiled up at him. “It isn’t serious, Sergeant. It looks like it gripped you by your pants and some skin but didn’t sever an artery. A miracle. I’ll just apply a field dressing.”

“Make it quick.” Tower hopped into a better standing position. “Anybody have eyes on it?”

“Negative,” McGary said.

“No,” Ryan said.

The rest of them shook their heads too.

“All of a sudden, I was on the ground,” Tower said, “pounding fists against warm steel.”

Ryan looked around. “Where’s Bates?”

There was no sign of the lieutenant. Either he’d run away or he’d been attacked. Except there weren’t any new blood trails to follow. Trying to contact him by shoulder radio would have been pointless. His had been removed.

First Moss had been attacked and was likely dead. Then Slater. And maybe Bates. Tower was still alive, but it was difficult to see him in such a state. He was the soldier who impressed in every way.

Ryan outranked Tower, but secretly Ryan wished someone like him had been in charge after the A-brid crashed.

But that was before he was attacked.

It was going to be even more slow going now. No way around it. In order to do everything to standard—no man left behind, including the dead—would add days to getting back to base. Maybe even weeks.

They had water, could find more and purify it, and they had food. But so much had gone wrong and the more time they spent out in the elements, the more times the shit could hit the fan.

Tower stopped, pushing gently on the dark dressing across his leg. "Leave me here."

Ryan almost laughed. "That's a big, big negative, Sergeant Tower."

"Think about it. We go this pace, we'll encounter everything with teeth. It planned this."

"Planned what?" Burbano asked. "Obviously, man, but which part?"

"I was chosen. I'm the best of you, I don't mind admitting it with Moss missing. I slow down, we slow down. This thing is going to use my injury to hunt us down one by one. Slater got slaughtered. Maybe Moss did too. The lieutenant is missing. You're all next unless you do as I say."

Others objected too, but Tower raised a fist.

"There are no officers here, just us. I'm including you McGary. Hot shot pilot or not, you're one of us."

"I appreciate that," McGary said.

"I'm not going to get you all killed. I won't. I refuse. Leave me and you have the best chance at survival. Period."

"And if someone else gets attacked, but they live, or some other injury, we're supposed to leave them too?" Ryan asked. "Would you?"

"This has nothing to do with rank. You know I respect you, Sergeant Ryan, but shut up and do it."

"No." Ryan had to look up even though Tower was slumped. "There is no *you*, only *we*, and *we* are a squad. Understood?"

"Yeah," Page said.

"Sergeant Ryan couldn't be more correct," Newlin said.

"Get real," Burbano said.

"We got you, Tower," McGary said.

Tower would have definitely argued, but he was in no shape to do so. He was pale, he blinked too much, and he looked like he was about to fall asleep standing up.

"How do your wounds feel?" Ryan asked. "Be honest."

"They hurt like a bitch."

"Good. And what is pain?"

"Weakness leaving the body."

"That's right. Pain will keep you going. And alive. You want to take a hot shower when we return to base?"

Tower exhaled, grinning. "Actually, I want to soak in an ice bath."

"Well, what are you waiting for?"

Tower inhaled and exhaled, straightening his drooping posture. "Yes, Sergeant. But I have a suggestion."

"Yes?"

"The dead. You know what I'm about to say. They don't call us Iron Sights for nothing."

It had been on Ryan's mind too. And probably it had been on everyone else's as well. In order to remain as fit to fight as possible, they needed to stay as lean as possible, and that meant making hard decisions.

Ryan glanced around. "We leave the body bags. Outsmart this thing. Make it so, it can't use our humanity against us. We'll return for them once we get back."

"I'll fly you there," McGary said.

CHAPTER 20

While aboard the A-brid, having transformed into a helicopter after jet formation, the ground had been a blur as it thundered above it, before Swain ordered the door to be shut.

Ironically, they'd all wanted to get to the destination, where they'd planned on searching for those who were missing, quickly. The crash had changed everything.

The beautiful landscape was quite different when having to march the terrain. But then it always was. Soldiers learned that fact as early as basic training.

What had happened was so maddening, Ryan thought. A waste of time for such elite soldiers.

Had the A-brid remained airborne, they probably would have located the explorers. Or discovered a clue to their whereabouts. Ryan ignored thinking that they'd probably been eaten.

The explorers, them being alive or dead, the squad could have confirmed their status and returned to Fort Beckett by now.

Tower limped but kept up. "It could have killed me."

"Yeah, but it didn't," Burbano said. "Stay motivated. And count yourself lucky."

"I'm not lucky."

"How is being alive not lucky?"

"And also, we should have killed this thing already. We're the best."

"That's pushing it."

"I don't mean all of us, or of all time, obviously, my dad can outrun me, but after this many generations of humans; look at where we are. Look at what we're doing."

"What's your point?"

"My point?" Tower said. "Is that *they* sent their best too."

Ryan ignored the fear prickling the back of his neck, flushing down his arms and raising the hairs.

Tower increased his hobbled pace, increasing the pace of the entire squad in turn, since they wouldn't go any faster than he could.

"Whatever caused the crash, *it* ordered it to do it. To sacrifice itself. Another of its species maybe. But maybe the other species that McGary saw." Tower grimaced. "And instead of taking us on all at once, because of what it did to Moss and Slater, maybe Bates, and myself, now it can be patient. Now it can hunt us down one by one. Now *it* is in control."

"Whatever," Newlin said, "it's just an animal."

"So are we," Tower said. "This thing is like us; a stripped-down rifle, no attachments, no scopes, just iron sights. It's teeth and claws and wits, and that's what makes it so dangerous."

"There's gotta be more than one we're dealing with then," Burbano said.

"If there were then we would have killed it," Tower said. "There's only one. And this thing got deployed like we did. What it's doing is . . . it's familiar."

"Explain," Ryan said.

"It understands strategies and tactics. Most predators will go after the weakest first. I think Moss was a fluke and Slater . . . Slater was a competent soldier. Bates kicked my ass. I don't have to state the obvious, but I am not the weakest. Except by injuring me it has hobbled our momentum. And that's exactly what I would do. It wants us dead but also it wants to survive. What better way than to weaken the alpha?"

Tower wobbled. Ryan was alongside him, and held out an arm for balance, he waved away. "I'm positive we already walked over where the explorers disappeared."

Ryan eyed him. "And they did something with them. Hid them. Out of sight. Buried them or ate them."

"Affirmative. We make a stand until this is over . . . or none of us are going home. Maybe Bates was correct."

There was a growl. Something low and fierce. They all heard it because they aimed their weapons in the same direction.

"I hate that fucking grass," Page said.

Their aim aligned with the sound of something somewhere in all of that swirling green. Then whatever it was trampled through it at high speed.

The command to fire wasn't necessary because they all started shooting. There was a blinking wall of muzzle flashes.

Whatever it was, it was so fast that Ryan barely saw it. It was very similar in shape to predatory cats from Earth, just bigger and the wrong color. It was blueish with dark stripes.

The soldiers continued to shoot, some aiming where the trampling was coming from, others ahead of it, and even behind it.

For some reason, it sounded like it was in front of them but also behind them. The sound of it running and all of its commotion was echoing off of the nearby hills, and the denseness of the grass was tossing sound everywhere.

Ryan stopped shooting. "Cease fire!"

Ryan's fellow soldiers continued to shoot where they believed its tail, paws, jaws, and speed to be.

"It's trying to get us to run out of ammo! Cease fire, dammit!"

There were a few more pops of gunfire but eventually everyone did as Ryan had commanded.

"It wants us low on ammunition," Ryan said. "It wants us to shoot at it. No one fires until it's in plain sight. Tower, you're right. Establish a perimeter. We're not going any further until we kill it."

Tower cleared his throat. "It isn't human, so it can probably track us by scent alone."

"What the *hell* are we supposed to do about that?" Burbano asked.

"Men," McGary said. "I don't think we should say our plans aloud anymore. I think it can understand us."

Ryan wasn't sure if he agreed with that or not but he trusted McGary. Maybe they should speak cryptically. Give them something to work on, training while on a mission that maybe they could implement in the future.

Can't hurt.

Lessons learned during a mission were often applicable during future ones. Ryan was about to reinforce McGary's suggestion by a command when the bugs went quiet.

The bugs had started up again after the shooting was over. But now it was like they all disappeared all at once.

McGary pointed a quivering finger instead of aiming his weapon. "Look out!"

It was too late. A dark pill-shape the size of a man flung toward them. On one end were jaws clamped tight. The thing had launched into view, advancing on them before they could fire another shot.

Newlin tripped over something, fell, and didn't move.

Incredibly, it was one of the body bags in its jaws. It swung it full force into Tower and his head snapped to the side. Ryan heard his neck break before he collapsed to the ground.

It pounced onto Tower, and even though he was clearly dead, it closed its jaws over his face, biting hard, crunching bones, then ravaging him by shaking it back and forth. Tower's large body flopped around as if it weighed nothing.

No one fired their weapons because they would have shot Tower. Everyone must have known he was dead already but they couldn't be sure and the creature was using him as cover.

The entire time the thing peeked out and glared at Ryan, predatory eyes reflecting, as if understanding him to be in charge. Ryan had experienced defiance enough times from humans.

A big fuck you to me, and the rest of us.

Ryan wanted so desperately to kill it, but the way it had positioned itself meant he might have accidentally shot a compatriot. Tower, dead or alive, Ryan couldn't be sure, and it kept moving him around.

When it released its bite, the impressive soldier Tower had been was unrecognizable. The middle of his face was gone. What remained of both sides were mushed together from the power of its jaws. His head was crushed. There was so much blood.

Then it went after the rest who'd grouped together. It took swipes with its claws, slicing right through Page's throat, and it rammed its snub face into Burbano's midsection, digging under his LBV.

Ryan didn't have to guess that it was chewing. Burbano's hollering expressed as much, but once again Ryan couldn't shoot it without shooting a compatriot, and Ryan couldn't shake the feeling that it wanted that to happen.

McGary had frozen. He snapped out of it and tried running forward but he dropped his weapon and tripped over Newlin just as the creature mauling Burbano whipped its head to the side; taking flesh and blood with it.

Burbano was dead, and it disappeared again.

It had planned the attack, and it had happened right after McGary had suggested to keep their plans classified.

Ryan finally pulled the trigger, but it seemed he was shooting nothing except the forest of grass, so he ceased fire after a few controlled bursts.

McGary had righted himself and aimed his weapon again before lowering it. "The hell with this!"

He ran to where Ryan had been shooting moments before, holding a laser torch. He ignited it.

"Chief, no!"

As McGary extended the white-hot flame toward the swirling green, it appeared again. McGary should have been aiming his weapon with a finger on the trigger, not being so confident in the ability to make fire.

The hand holding the torch disappeared inside its jaws at the wrist, and with a twist, the flame fell out and shut off.

McGary screamed, and before he could do anything about it, like aim his weapon or pound his fist against it, it yanked him into the grass.

"It's got me!"

McGary's voice dropped off a cliff and then he sounded like he was being choked.

Ryan trudged into the overgrowth. The thing was slightly in view as it bit McGary by the throat.

Ryan put it in the sights of his Rovla. So did Newlin, who'd joined alongside him. The medic had regained consciousness.

McGary was dying or dead, so they both aimed, ready to end it, when Ryan sensed something behind him.

Maybe another one of those things. Maybe Tower had been wrong and there were more than one of them.

He glanced quickly to see it wasn't something but someone. Tower hadn't been wrong.

Bates wasn't zip-tied anymore and shot Newlin in the head. Then he swung the Rovla assault rifle by the barrel, ignoring its heat in his hands, something only a madman would do, striking Ryan alongside the head with the flat of the stock.

CHAPTER 21

It was night, and the bugs were loud again, a wild concert enveloping Ryan as he was dragged by his boots. Before he could do anything about it, he was falling.

The ground punched up, and he landed on dirt. The wind knocked out of him, he rolled around on his back until he felt like he wasn't about to die.

When he stood up, he realized he was no longer wearing his LBV or helmet. They'd been stripped off of him. He was no longer armed with a Rovla assault rifle either, but he still had his boots on.

The hole looked to be about ten feet deep. The far side was a steep incline where there were claw marks, dug by some animal. But they didn't seem to be by the same creature that hunted them.

The claw marks were different than the imprint they'd seen. More herbivore than carnivore.

Ryan was about to call out but he held off. He'd been betrayed. That was all that mattered. He wondered if he was the only survivor. Other than who had thrown him down there.

Bates didn't show himself. He was probably just beyond the dirt rim, smartly remaining out of sight.

If he showed, Ryan would do his best to jump, scramble up the rim, grab hold of him, and pull him down there with him. Then see who was toughest.

Except what if he missed?

He likely would. Up was high and he would have to jump higher than he ever had in his life. Maybe fighting Bates wasn't the best plan of action.

Yet.

Ryan needed to figure another way out. It was hard to see clearly because it was night. Whatever considered the place to be its home, the ingress egressed in ways he couldn't identify, and there looked to be a spot darker than the rest. A tunnel maybe.

He reached out to feel how deep it would go, and it seemed wide enough for him to fit his entire body inside. Thankfully, he wasn't claustrophobic, or had developed claustrophobia as some soldiers did, having to keep the truth under their helmets.

If he climbed inside the tunnel and kept going, there could be a way out. But he withdrew his hand.

Planet Tuhrelevim was often breathtaking, but it was also alarmingly hazardous, and the predator hunting them wasn't the only one. No doubt there were other threats, smaller animals that could be poisonous, ones that hadn't been identified yet.

The last thing Ryan needed was to disturb some nest while underground when he was unable to escape. He might even get stuck. He had no doubt he'd definitely develop claustrophobia then.

Ryan began to regret being deployed to the planet at all. He was a soldier, and either he volunteered or went where they told him, but somehow he wished the foundation was solid before he'd arrived.

"Sergeant Ryan?"

Ryan couldn't see him. And he couldn't be sure what he wanted. Maybe speaking aloud would deepen the trap, and Bates would know where he was, precisely, so that he could shoot him.

But then why put me down here?

Remembering the darker darkness behind him, Ryan stepped backward, feeling cool air embrace him, and ignored that there might be something down there, watching and waiting.

"Staff Sergeant Ryan, I want to talk. This isn't a trick."

It was acceptable for a staff sergeant to be called sergeant, but Bates had used his full rank.

Respect or deception?

Knowing Bates as well as he did, Ryan knew the answer. He exhaled, considering what to do next, and as he did, Bates peeked into view.

The stalemate lasted nearly a minute. Both men hardly blinked.

"I'm sure you want out of there. Converse with me and perhaps I'll allow that to happen."

Ryan ignored the smirk on Bates's face and stepped forward into the dim light. "When did you lose it, man?"

"I've never thought clearer."

"Considering what you did?"

"If only the nickname of your pitiful squad was Plentiful Attachments Radios Tiny Egos Adelpa 3s And Shoulder Devils, and not Iron Sights, I wouldn't have had to take such drastic actions."

"If you say so."

"It saw me but did nothing."

"It? What did you do?"

"You know what I'm referring to. And it approved."

"It saw you do what, Bates?"

"Everything."

"You can't know what an animal is thinking."

"It isn't just an animal. And I do know because I ignored it, I never fired a shot in its direction, and I'm still alive."

"Even if you're right, it's using you."

"Being used is merely perception."

One thing Ryan knew, what he'd heard, was that crazy people didn't know they were crazy. That must have been true in Bates's case. Ryan had hoped there was some kernel of sanity in Bates somewhere during the previous days, but he'd abandoned the notion.

"You think it approves of you because it told you?"

"Don't be ridiculous. I observed it along the way. It showed itself to me. Our secret. A magnificent beast. Armor that gallops. That's what's out there. There's no defeating it."

"We could if we were armed with Shoulder Devils as you said."

"Join us. It's the only way."

Join us, huh? And to what end?

Bates had murdered Newlin. He probably would have killed the others if they weren't dead already.

He could have done the same to Ryan, and Ryan wondered what Bates's game was. He couldn't figure it out but he was sure Bates needed him for something.

Looking up, even if he could climb his way out—before Bates shot him—it would take him a minute. The best way to survive, it seemed, was to go along with a madman.

Ryan decided a dash of rebellion would reinforce his plan better. No matter Bates's mentality, he was smart.

"Defect you mean," Ryan said. "Betray my own species. Get me out of here and I'll consider it."

"No, no. Agree to join us now and I'll let you out. Not before."

What choice do I have? "I'm listening."

"Good. Tribes invade and conquer fellow tribes. Would you agree?"

"OK."

"It happened on Earth and it's happening here. Only we're not going to take anything. We're not going to obtain what we want, what the deep pockets supporting us desire. Anyone who remains here will die no matter what is done. Unless."

"Where is it now? Do you see it?"

"It's above us on that ridge." Bates motioned. "Do you see? No, of course you don't. You can't. Not from down there. You must be getting cold."

Ryan was shivering. "Spare me the nonsense."

"Spare me the nonsense, sir."

"Just tell me what happens next, sir."

"That is up to you."

"OK."

Bates cupped his ear. "OK?"

"OK, sir. I'll join you."

"Do you have any weapons?"

Ryan held up his filthy hands. "Just these," he lied.

CHAPTER 22

The two-man team that was reluctant but relying on each other turned out to be necessary for both of them. They hadn't gone far but it was far enough for Ryan to think straight. At first, he'd been relieved when Bates had pulled him out of the hole.

But Ryan had already accepted he'd been lied to.

He needs me to make it back. Help him with whatever command ordered, or used as a distraction. Then he'll turn on me as soon as base is in sight or sooner.

It wasn't as if Ryan had a backup plan, even though he should have. What options were there while trapped underground?

If he'd fallen into that hole by accident, he might have been injured, gotten stuck down there, and died.

Even though Ryan hadn't meant it, agreeing to side with Bates was the only way he could think of to survive. At least doing so kept Bates quiet.

Bates should have been aware of the possibility for deception, except he wasn't acting like it. Maybe that was how far gone he was.

Bates hadn't shot him, which he could have done easily; he was armed with a Rovla rifle, still holstered a pistol, and also, he had a knife. He wore an LBV, and a full rucksack bulged off of his back.

The beast was still out there somewhere, but it remained out of sight, and it wasn't the only threat; Ryan must keep a diligent watch over his final squad member.

Complete compliance seemed like something that would have agitated Bates, so because Ryan had been strategic, using defiance, maybe that was why Bates had believed him. Or believed Ryan long enough to help get him out of the hole.

In order for Ryan to stay alive, he needed to be himself. But who knew how long Bates actually planned on allowing him to live.

Since Ryan had been freed, and they'd been walking a while, he no longer wanted to pretend anything. "You're being manipulated."

Ryan pressed his thumb lightly along the sharp edge he'd taken from the A-brid, ensuring he gripped it right and didn't cut himself.

Bates hadn't noticed Ryan retrieve it from his boot, where the blade had been hidden, when he'd pretended to tie laces tighter a while back.

Bates looked at him. "What are you talking about?"

"It tricked you into helping it."

"Help it how?"

"By killing its enemies. Your fellow humans."

"I only killed one of you."

"Only?"

"With all of you dead, I will live."

"All of us. Why not leave me down there to die?"

"I changed my mind. I want it to witness my complete loyalty."

"Why were you on board with Moss taking a shot at it?"

Bates thought about it. "I believe I thought that if it was killed then that one didn't deserve my loyalty. I was testing it you see, and it didn't disappoint me."

"You're insane. You're no leader. You've never been fit to lead."

"I disagree."

With the ruse over, Bates didn't try to shoot Ryan with the Rovla he carried, he flung it away while dumping his rucksack and slashed at his throat with the combat knife.

Ryan should have remembered how skilled Bates was at hand to hand combat the way he'd handled Sergeant Tower, but somehow Ryan blocked the knife with his own blade, but his makeshift blade got knocked out of his hand.

Ryan grabbed for Bates's wrist, getting a hold of it, and squeezed, trying to get him to drop the knife.

Bates made his other hand into the shape of a knife and chopped again and again, and Ryan felt the brittle bones in his hand breaking, so with all of his strength, he wrenched the knife loose from Bates's grip.

Ryan got cut but after picking up his fallen one he had two blades, and when Bates rushed him, Ryan slashed the edge across his arm, stunning him, and stabbed with the combat knife, plunging it into Bates's eye.

Bates cried out and sank to a knee. Then he toppled over onto his side and was still. The knife must have punctured his brain. Bates was dead.

Ryan still gripped the bloody edge. He went to the Rovla and hefted it up. Then he ensured it was loaded.

He went to Bates's corpse. He reached down and tugged at the combat knife, wiggling it loose out of the blood pooling in his eye socket.

CHAPTER 23

Ryan hadn't expected it, and in comparison, ironically, it turned out Bates's life had been more of a safety net rather than a danger.

The beast circled him, invisible in the high grass, but he knew it was in there. And it wouldn't allow him to go any farther. The threat of it, the barks and growls, sounded every direction he turned.

It's toying with me.

Until he saw it out in the open, there was nothing he could do about it.

Ryan didn't know where Bates had hidden his full battle rattle, so Ryan had thrown on Bates's.

They were about the same size, and Bates had prepared. He'd stuffed as much necessary equipment into the ruck as possible, including as many canteens that could be found. Even empty ones.

Ryan would fill them whenever he needed to and purify the water. He'd chugged half of a canteen after the fight with Bates. He'd been so thirsty. And he needed to stay hydrated.

The shit had hit the fan. Bates had found the laser torch and stuffed it in the ruck too.

"This is for Iron Sights. See how you like this, *fucker*."

Ryan ignited the laser torch and held the white-hot flame to the grass nearest to him. The orange heat was a welcome sight, and soon the flames spread, crackling and smoking as it ate up vegetation.

He backed away, the smoke pluming the more the fire burned, and he kept the Rovla at the ready. He was willing to burn the whole planet if he needed to.

It galloped, reacting to the smoke. Ryan only needed it to show itself for a few seconds.

Long enough for a few well aimed controlled bursts. Such close proximity, he would aim for an eye.

It must have known Ryan was the last of the squad who lived because it no longer stalked silently. In fact, it rampaged angrily. And, also it barked, snarled, and growled.

Using fire as a defense, Ryan was able to hustle away to flat ground. He felt a twinge of regret as the forest of grass had turned into a field of fire. He hadn't wanted to do that if he could help it.

Something else was coming.

Whatever they were, there were hundreds of them, and they poured down the hills like a patient avalanche. They were bigger than what had hunted them so far.

They were quadrupeds too but seemed to be a different species. They mostly were white with dark stripes and they didn't have tails. Some of them looked to be darker than others.

Not bluish with a tail and what had hunted and killed the members of Ryan's squad. Still, to him, they looked to be related. Similar to the similarities between the big cats on Earth.

The new ones that were advancing were probably what McGary had seen and mentioned while the A-brid was airborne, what he'd reported to higher after Swain had requested it.

Incredibly, they began putting out the fire by digging and clawing, the dirt tossing around in clumps.

The landscape was soon a misty wall of brown haze, and the brightness of the blaze was diminishing. There was only so much grass to burn where Ryan had set the fire.

The beast that had hunted them had hunted them alone. But it hadn't been alone; it was the tip of the spear, with reinforcements nearby.

The rest of what it was in command of had waited for its orders; those barks and growls.

Or maybe *it* served them. Maybe it had been deployed by them as Sergeant Tower had thought.

The truth of which species was in charge changed nothing for Ryan's circumstances, but it was additional intel to report to higher once he arrived back at base.

If I survive.

Ryan wished he was armed with stun grenades or explosives, but the catch of being a member of Iron Sights Squad was limitations.

Other than attempting to locate missing explorers, the secondary objective was to report necessary equipment and weapons for future missions.

Ryan's compatriots needed to be warned of everything the enemy was capable of, including the ability to crash aircraft.

It was a stretch, and it was in case he died, and it was likely no one would ever find it to see it if he did die, but there was a chance.

Ryan crouched and withdrew the makeshift knife, sinking the tip of it into the sandy dirt, and began to write.

Bring the big guns

Deploy ALL OF IT

He remembered how McGary described the ones putting out the fire had attacked an herbivore.

Beware of Ravagers

But, also, he remembered the ridge where Moss disappeared. The claw marks in the dirt and the missing helmet she'd claimed she saw.

The warning wasn't complete, he hadn't described the beast that had wiped out his squad, but he could have scrawled pages worth of intel on the ground.

It would have to be enough and maybe less was more. He just hoped the beasts wouldn't find it.

Ryan had been diligent remaining hydrated, and he'd never had to urinate so badly. It wasn't the time, but it gave him an idea. He needed to be lighter for the trek back to Fort Beckett anyway.

He just hoped it would work.

Even if they started nosing around, hopefully his scent would repel them. They were smart but they were animals.

Detaching everything of use off of Bates's LBV—like loaded magazines—he stuffed all of it into the rucksack.

He opened the LBV, stretching it as wide as it would go, and laid it over the message. The armor wouldn't have saved him if even one of them got teeth and claws into him.

Then Ryan unbuttoned his pants, pulled down his zipper, and urinated all over the LBV, and even on the dirt surrounding it, outlining it as much as possible.

Something behind me.

It was risky, but he squeezed out every drop.

CHAPTER 24

The grass wasn't so high there. A tail thrashed above the tips, back and forth before the rest of it pushed past the green.

Ryan hoped it couldn't read his mind and know what he'd done. He hoped his warning would remain undisturbed until seen by human eyes.

The creature had allowed itself to finally be in view. He wondered if he could kill it and have enough ammo to deal with the animals nearby long enough to escape. If not, he would have to reload quickly.

It was risky for most soldiers to be alone. Most were used to depending on compatriots.

Ryan decided to remain ammo disciplined. Choose his shots carefully with controlled bursts. If he didn't, and he was attacked while reloading, he'd be killed.

Like the hole Bates had thrown him into, it had come through a hole in the ground to reveal itself. Whether it had dug the hole itself was irrelevant; now Ryan knew where Moss's body was taken. And maybe the explorers too.

The thing wasn't clear at first as it was still nighttime. Just the muscular outline of its thick neck and powerful torso. But then two yellow eyes opened; practically coals burning parallel in the gloom.

A beast could be still and hidden all it wanted, but a predator's eyes shined. Reflected. It obviously knew that, and meant it had kept its eyes shut, stalking them by scent or by listening.

Probably both.

That was likely why it hadn't been spotted. Only when it wanted them to was when it did. That had been a tactic.

Remembering when it killed Tower, when Ryan saw its eyes reflecting, he realized it had kept them mostly shut when it was near them.

And McGary had been right. It did understand them, or understood enough, often keeping its eyes closed to avoid detection, to remain unseen as much as possible, allowing its natural camouflage to work.

Otherwise, one of them would have shot and killed it.

It must have listened to the explorers too, learning from them that its eyes reflected when they were open. Before it had killed them, and probably hunting them at night too. It had done this before.

Maybe that was why the A-brid had been crashed, so it could listen to them, learn more about its enemy—humans.

Every word they spoke, every action they took, gave it intel. The question was what it was capable of doing with that intel and what it was planning.

And now I must be eliminated so more humans will come.

That was what it wanted the whole time. Even where they crashed, next to all that grass, had been predetermined. The perfect spot for it to observe them, remaining practically invisible while it trained against them.

And also, it was a reconnaissance mission.

The arrogance to show themselves even before the crash. It was planned, them guiding where McGary flew the A-brid, to get away from the packs of them, leading right in front of a creature that was waiting to sacrifice itself.

Knowing what would happen, and that it planned on slaughtering them after the crash the entire time. After it was done with them.

When did it decide it was time?

It was probably when it finally learned the depths of what humans were capable of.

Damn you, Bates.

If only Ryan could warn higher so that they knew anyone who was sent would be led into a similar trap. Ensnared already without even knowing it.

Not just Iron Sights Squad, but the mission after theirs, and the one after that, and however many more there would be after them.

Hopefully, someone finds my warning.

The planet would never be under human control. Ryan could tell that just by looking at the creature before him.

His only chance at survival was to kill it before it got the chance to communicate its discoveries. That way Ryan could complete the mission, partly, and try to save everyone else, to warn them from coming there.

Tell them the truth.

It was too close for him to aim and pull the trigger now. If Ryan got lucky and killed the thing, there were too many of the other kind nearby.

They knew where he was. He could see them. Their hundreds of eyes reflected too. It wasn't as if he could outrun them. He was outmatched.

It glared with yellow, shining eyes, and from a snubbed face were large fangs protruding down out its mouth.

It was large, but not as large as what it had commanded to put out the fire. A steep rise of hard muscle rose up above powerful legs planted like trees that were as big around as Tower's chest.

Dark stripes ran parallel all over its light blue body except for where the stripes bowed; arrow shapes middling each stripe. The stripes helped camouflage it, pointing toward its muscular head and powerful looking jaws.

Jaws that dripped saliva.

"You can't possibly understand every word, but I know you understand tone, so listen up: I will not be the last human you'll fight."

It squatted lower, about to pounce, leaning on its muscular and powerful legs. It looked ferocious, but mostly Ryan sensed intelligence. A tail flipped eagerly.

Maybe he should have pulled the trigger already. Except there was something off. Why hadn't it rushed him? Why hadn't it attacked while his back was turned? It could have. It was fast enough.

Ryan needed to do something it wouldn't expect. And it expected him to raise the Rovla, aim, and shoot. Maybe that's what it was waiting for. What it wanted.

It probably saw it as a challenge. See who was fastest. Something else to further prove itself against the enemy. And in the end, even less ammunition to use against its kind.

The lives of every person on the planet was on the line. Them and anyone else who set foot here in the future. Every human was doomed unless . . .

If he aimed his weapon it would attack.

If he raised it even an inch it would attack.

The Rovla was his most powerful weapon against the creature, but it was useless, an anchor.

Armor that gallops, my ass. You're dealing with the first round in the chamber.

Staff Sergeant Ryan let the Rovla drop to the ground.

The weapon clattered noisily, causing it to rear back. Ryan pulled knife and edge. He would drive either blade through an eye and into its brain like he'd done to Bates.

He saw a blur as he charged, realizing he couldn't have avoided the swipe of claws.

Then Ryan was on the ground and being mauled.

In such pain, he wasn't thinking clearly, and pulled his helmet off and swung it, but the helmet was knocked away by a lightning quick paw punch; skittering out of view.

The length of his arm was on fire and it felt like his shoulder had shattered. His arm flopped uselessly, nearly having been torn off, and he could only pointlessly push against it with his other hand.

As jaws bit into Ryan's stomach, his high-pitched screaming was loud, but not as loud as the echoing roars of approval.

www.ingramcontent.com/pod-product-compliance
Lightning Source LLC
LaVergne TN
LVHW010452160826
845677LV00012B/2453

* 9 7 9 8 3 5 5 8 5 7 1 9 6 *